SPIN THE BOTTLE

Fast Times at Ridgemont Hall #2

SARA WYLDE

Published in the United States of America by Sara Wylde

Cover Art by Bad Unicorn

Ebook ISBN 13: 978-1-948001-12-0

Print ISBN 13: 978-1-948001-13-7

WARNING

This book contains themes of pan and bi visibility. Even pan and bi people who end up in an m/f HEA. Pee-pees will touch. If any of this causes you to clutch your pearls, neither this book or this series is for you.

New Adult at its core is about new adults finding themselves. A lot of that includes exploring their sexuality and who they are.

These issues are important to me as a human, an author, and a bi person. #loveislove

For Virginia Nelson
The shining light who burns away every shadow.

JAX

"I JUST DON'T UNDERSTAND how, after re-enacting *The Exorcist* in your room last night, she can even look you in the face." I moved my Monopoly piece across the board to Park Place. "I mean, I only saw you in your tighty whities after that kegger and I couldn't look at you for a week."

"That's because—" Matt handed me the card for Park Place "—you're a prude, Jax."

"There is a difference between being a virgin and a prude." I wrinkled my nose and added the card to my bounty.

I certainly wasn't a prude, oh no. I hadn't been able to look him in the face because he'd become instant grist for the fantasy mill. I'd fantasized about Matt once or twice, but it had been hot because it was taboo, not because he suddenly had a body like sin. (Which he did.) He was my best friend. I wasn't supposed to think of him that way and that alone had given me a little thrill. Twisted, I know.

Of course, there was the part where I'd had a crush on him in middle school, but that was a long time ago. So long, I could barely remember.

"Not at *nineteen*." He said it like it was a thousand years.

"Yes, I'm practically ancient." I rolled my eyes. "Besides, you know my mother got pregnant with me when she was sixteen. That will not be my life."

Matt rolled the dice. "You know, they have these things," he drawled. "I don't know if you've heard of them, but they're called *condoms*. You use them to keep from catching crotch rot and morning sickness."

"They're only effective ninety-seven percent of the time. Which means three percent of the time—" I pointed at myself "—they fail. I *am* the three percent."

"You are overdramatic."

"Me?" My brows rose. "Oh, Matt!" I cried in a breathy voice, a faux affectation of the woman who'd been in his bed the night before and would be there again tonight. My voice rose an octave, "Oh, Matt! Oh God! Harder, harder...." And yet another octave. I didn't think I could actually get as high as she had.

He laughed. "Okay, fine. I'll admit, she was a little over the top. I mean, I'm good, but I don't think it warranted calling me God."

I rolled my eyes again. "Jesus."

Matt shrugged. "There it is again, folks. And I haven't even touched her."

"I'm going to touch you. With my fist." I wanted him to stop talking about this because it kept reminding me of Fantasy Matt™ and he wasn't real. This was Real Life Matt who farted the alphabet and could burp the star spangled banner. No thank you.

"I like it rough."

I laughed. "Now see, if I was prude, I would've blushed."

"Actually, I don't think that's a bodily function you're capable of. You don't blush, you don't giggle, and I definitely don't think you'd ever make a sound like, what was it, demonic possession?"

"Certainly not." I'd have the good sense to bite my lip. I may have been a virgin, but I wasn't a complete newb. I'd done everything but The Deed.

"Of course, you don't know what you'll do until you try it."

"How do you know I haven't?" I looked up from the game. Oh, this was going to get me in trouble. So. Much. Trouble.

2

"You punched your card?" Matt's eyebrows crawled up into his hair. I was pleased to say he seemed startled.

"No. But there are other things besides punching the v-card." I eyed him critically. "You know that, right?"

He smirked. "Just how far have you gone, Miss Priss?" All interest in the game was gone and he focused on me with a keen intensity.

I told Matt almost everything. *Almost.* When he started having sex, and I hadn't, I stopped telling him about the more intimate parts of my relationships. Not that I'd had tons, but it seemed like he was part of an exclusive club I hadn't been invited to join. It made me feel hopelessly naïve to be going on about a kiss, or a caress, when he was doing everything after. So I just kept quiet.

And I didn't want to hear about his conquests either.

But neither did I like the condescending look on his face, nor did I like being called Miss Priss.

"For your information," I began in a sugary tone. "I have decided to punch the card."

"Oh really? Who's the special guy?"

He looked so smug, I couldn't help myself. "You."

He choked.

And I laughed so hard, I almost peed my pants. "You can breathe now. I was just kidding."

Matt cocked his head to the side. "Well, why not me?"

"First, you looked like a deer caught in headlights and now you're insulted? Only you, Matt. And anyway, I was kidding." I stared down at the board game, pretending to contemplate my next move so I didn't have to look at him.

"Yeah. About the me part, not about the doing the deed part."

"So? You're not a virgin. You tease me about being one. It's time to get it over with."

"Jax. Get it over with? Really? It should be special. With someone you care about."

"Why does it have to be special? Was it special for you?"

"That's different."

"Why? Because I'm a woman and you're a man?" If he came at me with that, I was going to have to light him up.

3

"Nice to see you've finally realized I am a man." He winked at me.

"Well, legally you're an adult." I smirked at him.

He snorted. "Be serious, Jax."

"I am being totally serious."

"Then answer my question. Why didn't you pick me?"

"Is this really a thing right now? Why do you *want* me to pick you? You're not into me and of course that's what every girl wants their first time to be: a pity fuck from her best friend."

He took my hand and I wanted to pull away. "It wouldn't be like that at all. It'd be... an experience for both of us."

"Nah. You didn't magically wake up with boners for me and the person I do pick will think I'm hot. You love me, but you're not attracted to me. I deserve better than that."

"You're not hot, Jax."

"Thanks?" I wrinkled my nose.

"You're beautiful."

His blue eyes were so incredibly earnest. If I let myself, I could fall the hundreds of thousands of feet down into their depths. But I knew better. Boy, did I ever know better.

"I know you, Matt. You just want me to pick you because I didn't." I pulled my hand away. "Want another beer?"

"Yeah, I guess. Maybe you're right. I just don't like being excluded from the process."

I got up to grab him another beer. Mostly, to put distance between us. "I wasn't included in your process. And I swear to god, if you tell me it's different, I'm going to smack you."

"Well, you would've been if I'd decided to just get it over with, as you've so delicately described it."

"Why do I have to be delicate about it?"

He made that face again. The one where he looked like an animal frozen in the oncoming lights of a semi. "You know, I'm just going to drop it. For now."

"Forever. I'll tell you about it after it happens. Can we please go back into normal territory now?"

"I don't think we were ever in normal territory. It's Friday night and we're playing Monopoly." He held up his hands when I narrowed my eyes. "I didn't say it was bad. I love our Friday night table top ritual. But most people our age are out doing other things."

"You mean like getting shitfaced and playing makeout games?"

"Hey, you don't have to come next weekend if you don't want to."

"Of course I do. Shae and I made a deal. I'll go with her to that party at Bear Lake and she'll go to Curiosity Con with me."

"I thought *I* was going to Curiosity Con with you?"

"I know. It sucks you're just being replaced everywhere." The look on his face was like I'd actually hurt him. We teased each other all the time and it was never serious, but I could tell I'd struck a tender place with something sharp. "Hey." I put my hand on his shoulder. "If the Grizzlies make the playoffs, it's the same weekend. I didn't want you to feel bad about ditching me."

"So you decided to ditch me first, huh?"

"Compassionate release?" I offered him a smile.

"Yeah, okay. I actually wanted to go with you, but you're right. If we go to the playoffs, I'll have to ditch. Plus, I'm intrigued to see what you'll do if we play Spin the Bottle or Truth or Dare."

I lifted my chin. "Anything you'll do."

"Oh really?" he snorted. "What if you had to kiss..." He was obviously trying to think of the worst person I would have to kiss. "Pandora."

"I'd do it, of course. I'd probably be crying on the inside, but I'd do it."

"That's kind of hot."

"Oh, is it? What if you had to kiss Conrad? You want me to store that up for later use?"

He looked from side to side, as if he was unsure of where he was. "I mean, I guess if that's what does it for you. Pose me in your head any way you want. What's a little fantasy between friends?"

I gulped. I didn't mean to. It was an audible sound. It's just... it hit so close to home. Too close to the secret I'd kept from him.

And he knew me too well. "What was that?"

"What?"

"Okay, I'll let you play it that way. This time."

"Play what?" I scoffed. I snorted. I deflected. "I have no idea what you're talking about."

"Uh-huh. Okay. Would it make it easier if I go first?"

"First? What?" Oh god, what was happening?

"Come on, let's just get it out in the open. I know you've thought about me like that. That's why you couldn't look me in the face after seeing me almost naked. It's okay. I've thought about you, too. It doesn't mean anything. We're all drawn to bodies that are shaped in ways we like. It shouldn't be anything to be embarrassed about."

My face was on fire. "I'm not embarrassed about anything." I took a drink. "Okay, you know what? Fine. I had a thing for you in middle school."

"What?"

"Oh, like you didn't know? It was ridiculous."

"I didn't know. At all. What was it you liked? I was skinny, awkward, and wearing head gear."

"So? It was like the biggest betrayal when you turned into Jock Boy."

Then he smiled wide and I could read the mischief on his face. "So, you were into me? Yeah, that's right. I know I got it."

"Oh for shit's sake, this is never going to die, is it? We're going to be old and our grandkids will be playing together and you'll be like, remember that time you told me..."

He raised a brow. "Um, yeah? Of course."

That wasn't as hard as I thought it would be. Oddly enough, I thought it would make things weird.

But nothing could outweird what he'd told me about... had he actually admitted to fantasizing about me?

I couldn't think about that too closely.

We were friends. The best of friends. And that's all we were.

All we should be.

It was my turn again, but the board held zero interest for me. For him, too, because he handed me his cards. "You've got Park Place and Boardwalk, plus all the railroads. I'm screwed. You win."

"I always win."

"I know. We should play something I'm good at next time."

I snorted. "You win at basically everything *except* Monopoly."

"I know. I stomped your ass at Scrabble last week."

"Don't remind me."

"It's because you go for the pretty words, Jax. You've got to go for the points."

"I know. I just can't stop going for 'mephistophelian' over 'zoo.'"

"Have you ever actually made 'mephistophelian?'"

"No, but it's a bucket list item."

"Of course it is. Only you."

"No, I bet there are a ton of people who have 'Mephistophelian' on their Scrabble Bucket List."

"I think you're the only human being who has a dedicated Scrabble bucket list."

"Maybe."

He looked at his phone. "It's still early. You want to Netflix?"

"It is your turn to pick. Pizza?"

"Of course. I've got to hit the gym hard tomorrow morning. I need my carbs." He patted his flat stomach under his t-shirt and I got a glimpse of the ridges of his abs.

No, those weren't abs. I mean, they were. But they were also *Matt.* Not eye candy. Or that's what I had to keep telling myself.

A tiny, traitorous voice in my head whispered something to me and the aftershocks ricocheted like gunfire.

Maybe you should just pick him.

Tell him right now.

I watched Matt has he ordered the pizza on his phone. When he noticed my scrutiny he smiled at me, and that was the face of my best friend.

So familiar, but new to me in a way now that I didn't want because of everything I couldn't have.

No thank you.

"Make sure you get pineapple on my half." I said it mostly just to fill the moment. To put my mind back on an approved track.

"I know. Pepperoni and extra cheese, pineapple on half. Like that's changed in the last ten years. Give me some credit."

"Well, you can't say I didn't tell you what I wanted."

Except maybe he could.

I was in deep shit.

MATT

I DON'T KNOW why I'm so obsessed with who Jax gives her V-Card to.

The only part of it that should matter to me is that it's her choice. That I do know. For some reason, I don't want it to be. I can't think of anyone who is good enough for her.

She's beautiful, smart, generous and even though she comes off tough as nails, and to be sure, she's one of the strongest women I know, her insides are soft and tender.

I guess I just want to protect her.

I can't save her from the world. I know that, too.

I never should've said anything about those fantasies, either. What the hell was I thinking? I heard her choke.

Now it was weird.

The summer before we'd left for college, we'd spent every second together. She'd spend the night at my house, I'd spend the night at hers. We'd fall asleep together on the couch after watching movies or playing video games and eating pizza.

We were always together.

There was a distance between us now. Like, literally, right now. She was sitting on the floor next to me, but she didn't lean on me, or put her legs in my lap. I wondered if all this talk about sex had made her uncomfortable.

We'd always been able to talk about anything, so I hadn't really considered I might've overstepped in a way that bothered her beyond our normal teasing. I couldn't have that. She was safe with me and I wanted to make sure I never made her feel unsafe or uncomfortable.

"Hey, sorry about earlier."

"What do you mean?" She looked up at me, her dark eyes meeting mine.

"Pushing you about choosing me. Telling you I'd thought about you. Like that." The words tasted sour and I felt like an absolute shit.

"Forget it. I took it for what it was." Jax shrugged.

"And what was that? Because I'm not sure I knew what it was." I laughed, but it wasn't funny.

She scooted closer to me and leaned on me. "Good thing I know you pretty well, huh? You just didn't want anyone to take my attention. You're a selfish little bastard and you've never had to share me. I get it. I hate sharing you with your girlfriends. Hate. It."

"I thought you liked Bree?" I put my arm around her. It felt good to have her close.

"I did. I still do, actually. I'm sorry you guys broke up. She's great. But I still hated sharing my piece of your time with her."

That made sense to me. More so than my brother's explanation of why I was suddenly fantasizing about my best friend. She was beautiful, with all of her masses of thick hair and her dark skin. Her long legs, and... well, obviously, she was gorgeous, but she was Jax.

"Good. So we've agreed we're both selfish assholes."

"Yep." She snatched the remote from me, even though it was my turn to pick the movie, and I let her take it. "So I think we should revisit earlier conversation."

"Which one?"

"Who would be the worst person you'd have to make out with if we played Truth or Dare?"

"I don't know why we don't just switch to Spin the Bottle. Then you know you've signed up for the make out game and there's none of this truth business to distract from the good stuff."

"You know, by your logic, we should all just play Seven in Heaven."

"Or maybe just draw numbers like the infamous Key Party that's happening Friday."

"I actually thought about going," she confessed.

I pushed down every ugly thing that made me feel and tried to remember to be her best friend. "Is that something you really want to do?"

"No, but yes?"

"Why? Tell me about it."

"Are you sure you want to hear this? It's dumb."

"It's not dumb. Tell me. I don't know why you think I don't want to hear this. Wouldn't you tell Shae?"

"I guess I would. It's just... I don't know. Isn't it weird?"

"Only if we make it weird." And I was doing a pretty good job of it.

"Again, I just want to get it over with, but not in a bad way. I want to have the experience and I want to... I don't know. It's silly, but I feel like this virgin status is holding me back from something. It's like the last wall I have to cross before adulthood."

"Uh, I hate to tell you—"

"—I know it's more complicated than that, but that's still how it feels to me. I feel like you're in a secret club that I can't join. It pisses me off."

"So this decision is just because you're feeling competitive?" That actually made more sense to me than the I-Just-Want-To-Get-It-Over thing. Jax had waited so long, and it seemed like such a change in character for her to go from being scared of all the possible consequences of sex to deciding to dive into the experience with someone she didn't know.

"No. See, it's complicated."

"I understand. Jax, I just want you to be happy. I don't think banging some rando will do that, but if you do, I'm here for best friend duty."

"Good. That's exactly what I wanted to hear." She wrapped her arms around her knees and started scrolling through the available titles. "I'm tempted to make you watch a Rom Com."

I didn't remind her that it was my turn to pick.

"Whatever." I really didn't mind them, those romantic comedies. I guess I was supposed to take offense and demand we watch something "manly." I was taught the manly thing to do was deal with your shit, and that's mostly what these movies were about: dealing with your shit and stepping up. What's not to like?

Unfortunately, she picked one about best friends who decided to try the friends with benefits thing.

If we were in a Rom Com, now would be the time to step up and own my shit, but we weren't. This was real life, and honestly, I didn't know *what* I needed to own. Only that there were a whole lot of complicated feelings about the situation.

At one point, she laughed and pointed at me. "That's you. Oh my god, that's so you."

I rolled my eyes, but smiled at her.

When the inevitable separation happened, she cried, and as per usual, I rubbed her back and she scooted closer to me.

"You know it's going to be okay. You watch these things because they always have a happy ending."

"I know." She sniffed. "But why is there always a hard part? Why can't they just look at each other and say what they're feeling? Why do they have to break each other's heart before they can be together?"

"Because people are incredibly fallible. We're all stupid when it comes to feelings, I think."

"You're right. Completely stupid."

I got the idea she was talking about more than the movie, but I didn't know what and it scared the shit out of me.

"Matt?"

"What?" I was really proud of myself that my voice didn't squeak.

She curled in closer to me, her head on my chest and I held her tight. In that moment, my impervious Jax seemed so fragile, so breakable. She never seemed that way before. Not even when she cried in movies. This was something else.

A surge of something I couldn't name washed over me and held her tighter.

"I have to tell you something."

"You know you can tell me anything." I rested my chin on the top of her head.

When she exhaled, her whole body shuddered and suddenly, I realized we were standing on some kind of precipice and whatever she said next was going to push us over the edge.

"I know who I'm going to pick."

I swallowed. "Yeah? Who's the lucky guy."

"Sebastian Rathbone."

The name was a kick to the gut. I don't know what I expected, but it sure as shit wasn't that.

"What the fuck?"

"I knew you wouldn't approve, but he ticks every box on my list in what I wanted out of the experience."

"It's not that I don't approve—" Actually, it *was* that I didn't approve. She could do so much better. "—I just..."

"Just?"

"You can do better."

"Can I really? I mean, I think he's pretty great. He's a manwhore, but he's honest about it. He's good at what he does—"

"How do you know he's good at what he does?"

She still didn't look up at me. "Women talk. I've heard things." Jax coughed. "Anyway, he's actually a nice guy."

"Have you ever talked to *him*?"

"Uh, no. I was getting to that."

"Okay." I mean, what else was I going to say?

"Okay? That's it? You don't have anything else to say about it? I know you have opinions."

"And you made it clear that you were not in need of those opinions. Just my support. So that's what I'm doing."

"Fine. Give me your opinions."

"That guy? Seriously?" I blurted.

She laughed. "Yeah, I guess that guy. I don't want it to be complicated, and it wouldn't be."

"You mean catching feelings? Jax, you might get confused anyway."

"I might, but I've got you and Shae to straighten me out."

"Okay."

"Is that the new gold standard when I say something you don't like? Is it just going to be okay?"

"It's not my choice, so I guess it has to be, huh?" I tried to keep my tone light. I wanted to be supportive. I was probably failing miserably.

"I love you, Matt."

"I love you too."

She squirmed around until she was laying in my lap. "So now that you and Bree broke up are you going to date The Exorcist girl?"

"I don't know. We don't really have anything in common. It was just a thing." I shrugged.

"That sucks. But hey, that means I don't have to share you for a little bit. Better for me." She grinned.

"Yeah, obviously you need all of my attention right now because you're making terrible choices," I teased.

"So if you think I actually can't be trusted to pick my own lover, who would you pick for me?"

The question caught me completely off guard. I had no idea. If I was honest, I didn't actually want anyone to have their hands on her, and that was completely unreasonable. I knew I should probably examine the whys of that later.

"No shithead college student."

She laughed. "Oh, seriously? What then?"

"I don't know. A virginity auction?"

She snorted and sat up. "Are you insane?"

"I don't know. Listen, if you don't care if it's special or not, why not? You could get a million dollars or something. That would be some nice seed money. After you graduate, you could take a year and live abroad. You'd have a lot of freedom."

"My mother would literally end me."

"No, why would she have to know?"

"My luck, I'd get to be a headline or something. *Hollingsworth Student Auctions Virginity*. Yeah, she'd kill me."

"Is it your body or hers?"

She laughed again. "Oh god, don't turn my own ethos against me. There's belonging to myself and there's my mother. But who said it won't be special with Sebastian?"

I scrubbed a hand over my face. "Maybe it will be. I hope it is."

"Really?" She turned her face up to mine, her brown eyes hopeful.

"Of course I do."

"Would it be weird if I asked you to tell me more about your first time?"

"Nah. Remember, it's only weird if we make it weird."

"Was it awkward? I mean, you told me you did it, but it was like you just got the gold star for achievement. You didn't give me deets." She bit her lip. "I'm kind of scared. I'm scared to ask him. I'm scared to do it. But I want to."

I thought back to Anna Gaines. I'd thought she was the most beautiful girl I'd ever seen. I couldn't believe she'd talked to me, let alone agreed to go to Homecoming with me. We'd started dating and after six months, we'd done IT.

"Of course it was awkward. We were both virgins. I had absolutely no idea what I was doing. Brandon told me to watch porn, which was the worst advice ever."

"So what did you do?"

"Asked my dad. He just gave me a box of condoms and said good luck."

"Oh my god. I am trying to picture the look on your dad's face."

"It was pretty great. I think he really wanted to tell me to ask my mom, but that wasn't going to happen, so I was basically on my own."

"My mom gave me a book," she whispered.

"What? Oh god."

"She asked me if I wanted to be on birth control and she wrote me a script. Then she gave me a book on sex for beginners. I never really looked at it. I just shoved it under my bed. I was mortified. Being a doctor, she was just like...whatever. Ask me if you have questions."

"I guess *I* should've asked your mom."

She laughed. "Probably. She'd have bought you the same book and been all clinical and professional."

"You have to dig it out next time I come over."

"That's why I didn't tell you about it. I knew you'd want to look at it."

"Of course I do. And you should too. I can't believe you haven't already, being as Type A as you are about everything."

"I'm getting to it. I'd actually rather hear about real life experiences than read about it in some sterile medical text."

"The first time we tried didn't go well. We were trying too hard. I couldn't get in. We both felt like failures."

"Oh no," she said.

"Yeah. It was bad. It hurt her, but probably because I was a clumsy fucker. It wasn't until we decided not to do it that we just... we did."

"And then you were doing it all the time. I didn't see you basically for the next six months. Until you broke up."

"Yeah." I grinned at her. "After that, it was everywhere. All the time. I like to think I learned a lot."

"My mom said it's about being able to communicate with each other."

"I'd agree with that. Which is why..."

"Oh, are we back to that?"

"No. Just making a point. If you've never said a word to Bastian Rathbone, how are you going to tell him what you want?"

She looked pensive. "I think that might actually make it easier. I don't have to look him in the face ever again."

"That's a big deal for you. Why wouldn't you want to look someone in the face after you've been intimate with them?"

"I don't know. Because I'd think about whatever face they make when they... we..." She shrugged.

"Uh, yeah. Duh."

"This just isn't going to work. Maybe I should just stay a virgin forever. I mean, then for sure I will never get pregnant."

"You'll also never know what it's like to have an orgasm with another person. You'd be missing out."

"Maybe I'll wait until I'm thirty, which we all know is practically dead, and then I'll take you up on your offer."

I snorted. "Hey, I'm not waiting around forever. I want to get married, have a couple of adorable kids and a summer house. I won't be available to donate orgasms. Even to my withered up best friend."

How had it come back around to us having sex again? I needed to not think about that. Because like I said, I had thought about her that way, but only because it was taboo.

She snorted. "Well, you best remember if you haven't settled down by thirty, we're getting married. You promised when we were sixteen."

"Yeah, don't I know it." I grinned. "So you should save yourself for me."

She snorted again, and almost choked. "Not a chance. I plan on experiencing life. We need an even playing field. I mean, what if it's terrible and you could tell me that's how it's supposed to be and I'd have to settle for bad sex for the rest of my life."

"You're on dangerous ground here, little miss virgin."

"As if."

"You know how competitive I am. You just challenged my prowess and now I feel I have to prove it to you."

"I dare you." Then she bit her lip. "See? I'm competitive too. That's probably a bad idea, right?"

"Most definitely."

But I was thinking about it now. Obviously, we both were.

"I suggest we take this conversation up again when we're thirty."

"Bet." But I found my gaze drawn to the vee of her shirt, and the swell of her breasts. I found myself thinking about the way she felt when she'd curled up against me.

I found myself thinking of how beautiful she'd be in the morning light with her nails digging into my back while I wiped away any doubt she could ever have about how good I could make her feel.

Yeah, we were both on dangerous ground and I didn't know how to get back to where it was safe.

JAX

LAST NIGHT with Matt was the weirdest thing that had ever happened.

Things had taken a turn into unfamiliar territory. He'd been flirting with me. Teasing me. Talking to me in a way I'd never experienced.

And I thought I knew mostly everything about Matt Graham.

It was intimate.

I'd started thinking about him again in a way that clearly on the no fly list. When he was talking about his time with Anna, I'd been looking at his hands. Imagining what they'd feel like on my skin.

I'd also kept thinking about how offended he'd been that I hadn't asked him.

If I wanted things to go that way, if I wanted his hands on me, all I had to do was say, I choose you.

But I wasn't going to.

I knew that sex was temporary. Lust was temporary. I was more concerned about what was after that. We'd inevitably fall apart. I wasn't naïve enough to think that we'd cross that line and then live happily ever after. We were both still so young and we had a lot of hurdles ahead of us.

No, if that line were to ever be crossed, maybe like I said. When we were thirty.

If I was honest, that wasn't too far away. And it wasn't anywhere near dead, like I thought it was when we were sixteen.

It was best to stick to my original plan with Sebastian. Of course, that meant I would actually have to talk to him.

Which was where I was headed currently.

Shae had texted me to tell me there'd been a Rathboner sighting in the library and I was off to find him. Of course, I wasn't quite sure what I'd do when I found him.

If I was honest with myself, I'd probably run away.

When I found him, his long legs were propped on the table, his ankles crossed, and he was patrician nose deep in The Bell Jar by Sylvia Plath. It didn't surprise me. He kept his arsenal well-stocked and what better way to seem like a sensitive, misunderstood, heart-of-a-poet type than to have intimate knowledge of Plath?

For all I knew, maybe he really did have the heart of a poet.

He looked up over the book at me, one perfectly groomed (oh my god, he had to wax to get that arch) eyebrow cocked.

"Yes?" he asked.

Well, this wasn't going as planned. It's not like I'd been staring at him hard enough to drill holes in his head. I wasn't ready to talk to him. He was Bastian-Fucking-Rathbone and I was...me. Which wasn't a bad thing to be, but I was aware my social skills weren't exactly up to par.

His hard perusal burned like staring at the sun. I found I couldn't move my mouth to form words. *Way to go, Jax. First mission: Failed.* Although, I expected to fail, so it really wasn't any kind of loss.

"Get back to me when you make up your mind." He turned his attention back to the book.

"I was studying you," I blurted. *Well, no shit.*

His eyes darted back up to mine over the rim of the book. "Were you, now? Are you an artist? Should I strip naked so you can draw me like one of your French girls?" he said, mocking Rose's lines from *Titanic*.

"I don't care for French, actually." Did I really just say that? It had nothing to do with French *girls*. Or the naked drawing of them. My palm fairly itched to smack my own forehead.

"Hmm. No? So you don't like romance languages in general?"

If only he knew. "No, not really. I prefer something more guttural, like Russian or German."

"Why is that?" He slipped a bookmark between the pages and closed the book.

"Lies are pretty. The truth is hard. It seems easier to lie when the words just roll off your tongue. I generally think that's why they call them 'romance' languages."

"Not a fan of love, then? Who shat in your cornflakes? I don't *think* it was me..." he trailed off, seeming to be trying to remember if he'd already been in my panties.

"No one shat in *my* cornflakes per se, but I've seen what it's done to others."

"Which brings us back to the original question."

"You didn't actually ask a question. You answered one. You said yes."

He smiled indulgently. His teeth were so white he could've been a model for a toothpaste commercial. "Allow me to rephrase. What have I agreed to?"

I sighed heavily, debating if I should simply put all my cards on the table, so to speak. Even the V-card. The good thing about having no social skills to speak of, or the bad thing depending on how you looked at it, was that my mouth opened and words fell out before I could fully contemplate the aftermath of the bombs I dropped.

"Punching my V-card. But I haven't decided if you're the one to do it or not." Obviously, I had, but I needed some sort of mystery.

As soon as the words left my mouth and a look of surprise bloomed on his face, I wondered if maybe I should have some kind of filter installed to save myself from future humiliation. I mean, what could he say here? Oh God, what if he laughed at me? I should just rip out my tongue and slap myself with it.

"You're not sure?" He laughed, but he didn't seem to be mocking me. "Well, it's been awhile since I've had to give the sales pitch. I might be a bit rusty. But you've read the fine print?"

The sales pitch? I rolled my eyes. What a dick. But of course, his dick was all I wanted him for, so I wasn't going to judge. Or I'd try not to, anyway. This was much more complicated than I'd thought.

I could only assume he meant the "no strings attached" clause. "I'm on board with the fine print. That's why you're at the top of my list. I really just want to get it over with."

He smirked. "You make it sound like ripping off a Band-Aid. If that's really how you feel about it we can go back to my dorm right now. Band-Aid ripped."

"That easy, huh?" Butterflies swarmed in my gut. I could do this, right now. Mission accomplished. Only, there was this little voice in the back of my head that said I should wait. I don't know what I was waiting for, but that voice was usually right.

He cocked his head. "That easy."

I swallowed hard. "That's good to know. But if you'll recall, I hadn't decided yet."

He sat up and turned to face me, the book forgotten. "What's the deciding factor?" Bastian asked me, as if he were talking about something as inconsequential as the weather.

"Well, I have this list—" I began.

"Really? Do tell." He looked over at me as if I were some kind of new bug and he'd just managed to slap me on a slide.

I realized I hadn't even told him my name and we were talking about punching cards and my list. At least I hadn't told him my mission statement.

"I don't think so." Suddenly, this seemed wrong and I wanted to escape his scrutiny, but my feet were rooted to the spot.

"Oh no, sweetheart. You opened the door and invited me in." His eyes narrowed with predatory delight.

"You don't even know who I am. Why should I tell you anything?"

"I don't know." He made a show of shrugging. "Why would you put me at the top of your list, *Jax*." It wasn't really a question.

I'd walked right in to that one, but I brushed it off. He knew who I was. That was the most important thing here. What could it really hurt to tell him? I'd already admitted he was at the top of the list. He was willing to do it and wanted to know about his competition. So in for a penny in for a pound, right?

I sucked in a lungful of air. "Fine. I have a list with three candidates. I'm currently evaluating them for suitability."

"Requirements?"

I didn't actually have any requirements. I just picked two guys I was attracted to and the third... I scrambled for something to say. "The candidates have to be attractive, know what they're doing, and then they have to go away."

"Don't you want it to be special?" His expression softened.

"Why does it have to be special just because I'm a girl? You sound like my friend, Matt. Jesus Christ."

"It should be special just because it's your first. Girl, boy, either, neither, or both."

"Interesting you have that opinion. I thought you were just a manwhore." I couldn't believe I'd just blurted that out. He probably thought I was Queen Spaz of Spazmania.

"Manwhores have rites of passage, too. Someone had to be my first." His voice had dropped to soft timbre that wasn't exactly a whisper.

"And was it special?" I asked, not really expecting an answer.

"No. It wasn't." His eyes were suddenly hooded and dark and it occurred to me that maybe Bastian Rathbone was more than the caricature he'd made of himself.

Of course, those were dangerous thoughts. I couldn't let myself see him that way, not if he was going to be the one. Strictly business.

"So who else is on this list of yours? Maybe I can help you decide." The devil-may-care mask was back in place.

And honestly, that was just where I liked it.

"I'm not sure I should tell you."

"I'm intrigued. How about dinner tonight and I'll try to convince you?" He smiled again and I thought about what it would be like to kiss him.

"It's not Friday. You only take out your new girl on Friday."

"You said you hadn't decided, so your week hasn't begun. And Friday is the party at Bear Lake. I think we'll both be busy, won't we?"

Another question erupted from my mouth that probably shouldn't have. "My week? Can any woman who wants you have you, or are you actually attracted to me? I mean, I don't want to be the pity screw." I recalled saying something similar to Matt just yesterday.

He looked pained. "Christ, but you're brutal, aren't you?"

"I'm just honest." I shrugged.

"No, there's honest and then there's you."

"Are you going to answer the question?" I cocked my hand on my hip.

"If you tell me who else is on your list."

"I thought dinner was the bribe for that information?" I narrowed my eyes as I assessed him.

"It can be, but I wanted to spend more time with you."

"Why?" My eyes narrowed further, so much so, I was practically squinting.

"You intrigue me. You have since Statistics."

He wasn't dropping some crappy line on me, we had that class together first semester.

"Why?" I repeated, eyes widening now. I probably looked like a startled owl.

"You say whatever is on your mind and you don't care what other people think of you."

I snorted. "You don't seem to care what other people think of you, either."

"So I guess we have that in common." He smiled, but it didn't reach his eyes.

"Here's the thing, if this is going to work, if it's going to be you, then we can't be friends."

"Maybe it won't be me. Like I said, you intrigue me. And I don't do strings."

Hadn't I just said *I* didn't want any kind of attachment?

"What happened to we could go to your dorm right now?"

"Changed my mind." He stood. "I'll pick you up at *your* dorm at seven."

And like any good romance novel hero, he made his exit, leaving me to wonder if that had actually happened.

I replayed the whole thing in my head about a hundred times in the span of five minutes. Yeah, it happened. I'd opened my mouth and stuffed my own foot as far down my throat as it would go.

Tonight, I'd be hanging out with Bastian Rathbone. Dinner, he'd said.

Panic surged. I couldn't go anywhere with him. I hadn't planned on having any actual conversations. Or hanging out. Or dinner. Or... Oh god. I had to call Shae. I needed a better plan, this one wasn't working.

He didn't even know which dorm I was in. Did he?

I was officially freaking out.

"You look like that time you drove over a squirrel in driver's ed."

I was startled to see Matt standing in front of me. Definitely Queen Spaz of Spazzmania.

"No, it's infinitely worse than running over a squirrel. The squirrel didn't know to look for a Mack truck. I do."

"What did you do?"

I suddenly didn't want to tell him that I'd moved forward with the plan. I thought about last night and a cold chill of guilt washed over me. But that was dumb. Right?

Bastian saved/damned me when he appeared out of nowhere and said, "It is Ridgemont Hall, right?"

"Right," I breathed. My voice was high-pitched and breathy, and I sounded valley girl vacuous. It was gross, but I couldn't seem to stop doing it.

"See you later." I didn't know three non-sexual words could sound so...so... I don't know, like a promise. My stomach did strange things, flipping around like some kind of circus act. "Oh, and—" he paused to look Matt up and down, and finding him lacking, continued— "bring your list."

Bastian wandered out of the library this time, his gait slow and leisurely.

"So you're really going to do it?"

I nodded.

"Okay."

I'd started to hate the way he said okay. I still felt the weight of his disapproval.

"I do have another option for you to consider. You asked me last night and I thought of someone."

This should be great.

"Who?"

"Brooklyn Chase. He's been asking me to introduce you for a while."

"How long is a while?"

"Since practice started this summer."

"You dick. Why didn't you introduce us? He's hot."

Matt frowned. "If you're into jocks, which it seems like you are. How did I not know this about you?"

"I don't know that I'm specifically into jocks, but that's where all the manwhores are."

"Brooklyn is not a manwhore."

I laughed. "Aw, you're defending his honor."

"You know what, I am. He's a good person. I think you might actually like him."

"Which defeats the purpose of a one night stand, now doesn't it?" I crossed my arms over my chest.

"Yes. Let him get to know you. Get to know him."

I realized then that's what I was afraid of. I didn't want to fall in love. I didn't want to be tied down to the first person I shared my body with. "That's not what I want, Matt."

"Okay."

"Goddamn it," I growled.

He laughed. "I'll keep my phone on if you change your mind and need a rescue. Usual code."

For minute, I considered. "Do you think I'll need a rescue?"

"No. I don't actually have anything against Sebastian except I think he's not good enough for you."

"Who do you actually think is good enough for me? Don't say Brooklyn, because for some reason, you didn't want to introduce us when he asked."

"No one. And like we agreed, we don't like sharing each other."

I laughed. "I guess you're right about that. But I've never tried to —" Except that was a lie. Senior year, Becky Grant. God, I hated her.

"Yeah, I'm glad you caught yourself before you could lie. You basically told me you'd never talk to me again if I went out with Becky."

"I know. But she was a shitty human being." I grinned. "And not nearly good enough for you." I winked at him.

"You're such a shit, Jax."

"I know."

MATT

SHE MAY HAVE BEEN A SHIT, but I was a first class bastard.

I don't know what my problem was, but I was being an utter tool.

Bastian took her out to Paisano's, which was one of the best Italian restaurants in the city.

How did I know that?

Because I followed them.

They were seated out on the patio and I could hear every word they were saying. I wasn't sure if that was better or worse.

I did know, however, if Jax saw my car, she'd kill me. Probably with her bare hands.

I couldn't help myself.

"I have a confession to make," Jax said.

"Already?" Bastian replied. He leaned forward and focused all of his attention on her.

She looked down at her hands and gave him a soft smile that caused an arc of jealousy to cut through me like a sword. My stomach felt like I had the flu.

"I didn't really have a list of people. I had a list of what I wanted from the experience and that came up you."

I was proud of her for being so brave. I couldn't have done what she did, but I was still pissed off she'd chosen that guy. I argued with myself that ultimately, it was her choice, even if I thought it was the wrong one.

"Why is that?"

"Because of your 'fine print' and I've heard you know what you're doing."

"So why didn't you come back to my dorm?"

"I don't know how to start. I'm scared."

Jesus, she was being so raw. So naked. I felt guilty for watching this moment because it wasn't mine. She hadn't given it to me. Yet, I still couldn't look away.

"It doesn't have to be hard, Jax."

"Doesn't it?" She smirked.

"Okay, you know what I mean." He was so gentle with her, that it made me realize I'd misjudged him.

And myself.

I knew I should drive away. I should wait for her to tell me what happened. To give me what she wanted me to have, but I was riveted.

"Come here," he said.

"Right here?"

"Why not right here?"

Jax pushed her seat back slowly and stood. Even from this distance, I knew her hands were trembling.

I didn't want to see what came next, but it was like a train wreck. I couldn't look away.

He pulled her into his lap, and no one around them seemed to notice, or if they did, they didn't care. Bastian cupped her cheek, and kissed her.

My gut roiled, but I kept watching.

"Hey fucker, what are you doing?" Shae opened the door to my car and plopped, unceremoniously into the passenger side. "Oh. Are you here on BF duty in case she needs an extraction?"

I was tempted to lie, but I didn't. "No, I'm just being creepy."

She laughed. "Nah, you're just looking out for your bestie. It's your job."

"It's nice of you to think so, but if she knew I was here, she'd kill me."

Shae leaned over me to peer out the window. "Sebastian Rathbone? What?"

"Yeah. I have to say, I don't approve."

"I... let's go get coffee."

She'd offered me the out that I needed, even though I didn't want it.

"Or we can sit here and watch your bestie make out with my nemesis. Whichever." She shrugged.

"When you put it that way..." I started the car and drove to The Black Dog.

"I bet you're having some complicated feelings about this, huh? I mean, of course you are, otherwise you wouldn't be creeping outside the restaurant. What were you going to do, follow them back to the dorm? Or charge in and carry her out over your shoulder?"

"Those are all pretty great ideas." I'd admit, throwing her over my shoulder and running away with her hadn't occurred to me, but I liked the idea.

"I have another idea for you."

"What's that?"

"You could talk to her. Tell her what you're feeling."

"I tried. Sort of. It got complicated."

"Everything is, eventually, isn't it?" Shae said as she ordered her coffee.

"No. That's the thing. Jax and I aren't complicated. We're best friends. I just want her to be happy."

"Unless the happy is with Bastian Rathbone?"

"That's just it, isn't it? He dates casually and then he moves on. He's going to break her heart."

"How do you know? She told me she doesn't want a romantic entanglement. Are you going to tell me that you know what she wants better than she does? Because if you do, I might have to kick you in the dick."

"No, I just..."

Shae eyed me knowingly.

"It's not like that."

"Okay."

I immediately understood why Jax hated my "okay." It pissed me off. Much like everything else these days. I had to get a handle on this. I wasn't that guy and I definitely didn't want to be.

"We talked about it last night. We're just both really competitive and really selfish. We don't like sharing each other's time. That's it."

"Okay."

"Damn it, Shae."

"What? I said okay." Except she gave me this shit-eating grin. "Maybe you guys should just fuck and get it out of your systems."

"I offered. She wasn't into it."

"What? Really?" She had to wipe her mouth because she choked on her coffee.

"Of course. How else will I know she's safe and her partner will take care of her? Me. It makes sense. Right?"

"What did she say?"

"Besides no?"

She shook her head.

"I need to rewind my brain. Reset it."

"If you're just friends, why does your brain need a reset?"

I didn't say anything. I just drank my coffee.

"So she's coming to that party at Bear Lake. You are too, right?"

"Yeah, she told me. She said you replaced me as her guest at Curiosity Con."

"Sorry about that, but if you go to the playoffs..."

"Yeah, I know. Now, I don't have to feel guilty about ditching her, since she ditched me first."

"Exactly. I'm actually excited to go. So yay for me."

"Then why did you make her agree to go Wyndham-Scott's house party?"

"Because I was hoping she'd meet someone and V-Card punching would happen organically. Maybe even orgasmically."

"Maybe it still will. Who knows?"

"Are you bringing anyone?" she asked.

"No. Probably not."

"Good. You can hang out with me. Although, we're probably going to play Truth or Dare."

"God, those games are so dumb."

"Shut up. Whatever. You still play."

"I know." I rolled my eyes. "I always say I'm not going to, but then I can't help myself."

"None of us can. So I just roll with it."

"I heard that it's the same weekend as the Ridgemont Key Party."

"Yeah. I'm not down to being Pandora Heyde's puppet. I'd rather find my own trouble, thanks."

"You and me both." Pandora Heyde was ruthless, and I shuddered to think what she'd be like as a full grown predator.

"Hey, how about a lift home?"

"Sure."

I took her home to her apartment off campus.

"Wanna come up and hang for a while?" she offered.

"Yeah. I do." Because I couldn't stop thinking about Jax. What she was doing right now. If she was going back to her dorm. His dorm. I couldn't get it out of my head.

Shae wouldn't let me do that to myself.

"We're baking cookies. Then we're gonna kill some shit on CoD. Good?" She unlocked the door and we went inside.

"We get to eat the cookies, though, right?"

"Of course we get to eat the cookies. What kind of dictator do you think I am?"

"Obviously, a benevolent one."

I followed her into the kitchen and she handed me a package of premade dough. "You get the chocolate with extra chocolate. Cookie sheets are under the oven."

"What kind do you have?"

"Peanut butter chocolate chip. Don't worry. We'll share."

That was something I liked about Shae. She didn't assume that just because I was a guy and a jock, I had no idea how to read the directions on the back of a pack of pre-prepped cookie dough. Or thought that I'd never done it before.

When I was in middle school and it was my job to bring cookies for the holiday party, my mother had taken me to the store and let me pick out the cookies, but when we got home, it was all me. There was no reason, she said, that I shouldn't know how to do that.

A couple of the guys in my pod had no idea how to do laundry and had no interest in learning. That baffled me how these fully grown adults could walk around with no idea how to take care of themselves and no interest in learning how.

After popping my cookies in the oven with hers, we set the timer and started a game of CoD.

Part of me kept waiting for Jax to join, but that would've been stupid. She was out on a date with Sebastian Rathbone and I was sure he did not play Call of Duty.

He was probably rereading the original version of Dangerous Liaisons in French out loud to her while he...

While he what?

What the hell is actually wrong with you? Stop.

It occurred to me that maybe I shouldn't go to the party at Barclay's this weekend. I should stay home and get my head straight.

After cookies. Definitely after cookies.

I'd finally been able to get Jax out of my head and I'd gone home when she texted.

Jax: *You busy?*

Me: *I'm gestating a food baby made out of cookies, but otherwise no.*

Jax: *You cookie cheater.*

Me: *I am. With Shae. We baked peanut butter chocolate chip and chocolate chocolate chip.*

Jax: *Rude.*

Me: *You know it. Wanna come over while I give birth?*

Jax: *You're so gross. Did you save me any cookies?*

Me: *I ate them. Every last one.*

Except I had a Ziploc that had four cookies in it we'd both saved for her.

Jax: *You liar. I know you saved me at least 2.*

Me: *Fine. 4.*

Jax: *You love me! I'll be over in an hour.*

I looked at time on my phone. It was still pretty early if things had... Unless it had gone poorly. While I wouldn't choose Sebastian for her, I *did* want things to go well for her.

Me: *So...*

Jax: *No. I'll tell you about it when I get there.*

Me: *Okay.*

Jax: *Damn it.*

Me: *What?*

Jax: *I just hate it when you say okay now. Shut up. So I can shower.*

Me: *I'm special.*

Jax: *Not really. I just smell like Sebastian's cologne.*

Me: *I don't care if you smell like his cologne.*

That was a goddamn lie if I'd ever told one, but maybe if I forced myself to smell someone else on her, I'd stop thinking she belonged to me.

Jax: *Coming.*

Me: *Obviously not, or you wouldn't be coming over.*

Jax: *Why do I talk to you again?*

Me: *You love me.*

Jax: *Maybe. If you're lucky.*

Me: *I am so lucky.*

Jax: *Yeah, you are. Now shut up. Wait, do you have milk?*

Me: *Obviously.*

Jax: *And a pair of those shorts?*

I had a couple pairs of these old shorts that were soft as fleece and she liked to steal them. I liked to pretend I wasn't going to let her.

Me: *Are you coming over or not? Haul your cookies or you're not getting these cookies.*

Jax: *...*

There was a knock on the pod door and I knew it was Jax.

I wasn't prepared to see her standing there.

Which was stupid. I invited her over. I knew it was her. And yet... there was something different about her.

Her lips were swollen, bee stung. Her eyes had a glazed look to them, and her smile was so wide and pure, it was brighter than the sun.

"Hey," she said, and bit her lip.

I opened the door wider and as soon as she was inside, she was looking for her cookies.

"Gimme," she said.

"Pay up," I said.

"With what?" She narrowed her eyes.

"Sugar for sugar. Right here." I pointed to my cheek.

What the fuck was I doing? Why had I said that?

Luckily, she didn't really notice. She leaned in, pecked my cheek and snatched the bag of cookies out of my hand.

She wandered into my room and opened the dresser drawer and pulled out her favorite pair of shorts and went into the bathroom to change.

This was such a bad idea.

Her ass. My shorts.

My dick was about explode out of my jeans.

"So, you still want details?"

"Yeah, of course." No, I didn't. Not really. I mean, I did. I wanted to be supportive, but I admitted to myself I wished it was me. Not just because it would be special, but because I wanted to kiss her. To make her glow like that. To put my hands all over her.

"It was just kissing, but..."

"It's not just anything. If it made you feel something, then it's important."

She rewarded me with another of those smiles. "You know what? I don't know why I was worried about telling you this stuff. You're exactly who I thought you were. My best friend. I hate that we had anything we didn't tell each other."

So of course, I felt like the lowest piece of whale shit. A big shit cloud floating in a sea of her praise.

"So he kissed you?"

"Yeah. It was kind of magical." She danced up to me and put her arms around my neck. "We were dancing like this." She spun around and I let her lead me into a dance around my room.

"Then what?"

"Then—" she dipped herself back "—he dipped me."

"Is that when?"

"Nuh-uh," she said, breathless. "Then he brought me back up oh-so-slowly. Holding eye contact. There was so much tension, I thought I was gonna die."

"Like this?" I brought her back up as slowly and precisely as she described and held her so close our heartbeats thudded together.

"Yeah," she sighed. "And then, bam!"

Jax dropped her mouth against mine for the barest touch. Her eyes flew open as it seemed to dawn on her what she'd just done.

I knew the thing to do was to smile, to ask her to tell what happened next. To take joy in her joy, to revel in the very innocent retelling of this moment she'd had.

But I didn't.

I held my gaze steady with hers. Held her locked against me, and she didn't move away. She was frozen.

I wish I could say I was frozen, but I wasn't. I was hot and hard, and I wanted her more than I've ever wanted anyone. Shockwaves of lust shuddered over me, like the hammering of a nail into the back of my skull and through my whole body.

Her lips parted and I saw something in her eyes that was like resignation. A surrender to the moment, to me. I didn't want to be something she surrendered to. I wanted to be what she'd chosen.

And she hadn't chosen.

This was a moment that had spiraled out of control.

"Then what, Jax? Tell me."

"I... I..."

"He kissed you?"

She licked her lips. "Uh-huh."

"Was it hard or soft? Was it everything you wanted it to be? Did it reassure you that you'd made the right choice?"

"It did." And I saw that resignation wash over her again. A certain flavor of fear. "Until right now."

I knew what I had to do. This wasn't about me and it never should've been. I pressed my lips to her forehead in a chaste kiss. "No, you made the right choice."

She tightened her arms around me and I focused not on the body that I held, but the woman, and what she needed from me.

What she'd asked for from me, which was only my support. She hadn't asked for my dick.

I'd been perilously close to crossing a line. It wasn't that we couldn't come back from it, of course we could. If a kiss could break us, we deserved to be broken.

I was being a selfish asshole. That's what it boiled down to.

"Now tell me why it was magic," I said.

"I think I just want to eat the cookies," she said, her voice low and soft.

JAX

Kissing Sebastian Rathbone had definitely been an experience.

Like I said, I'd been intimate with partners before. I just hadn't... Done the Deed, so kissing wasn't new to me.

But kissing the way Sebastian did it was.

It was so intense.

He'd made me feel as if the whole world had stopped on the head of a pin, and only he could make it spin again—and when he did—it was all for me. Or maybe that was me? I was the one spinning.

Until I'd screwed up and whatever that was had happened with Matt.

He looked at me in a way I've never seen him look at *anyone*. It wasn't the world that stopped that time, it was my heart.

But we both knew it was just Matt being competitive. Wasn't it?

He'd been so hard. Jesus, and I'd been pressed up against him so tight.

And it had been so good.

My whole body got hot thinking about it.

Then the fucker kissed my forehead and acted like it never happened. Which, to be honest, was probably the best idea. Except things were changing between us whether we wanted to admit it or not.

The only time I could stop thinking about his hands was when I was with Sebastian. I wondered if that would hold true at Bear Lake? Part of me thought I should just go ahead and follow through there. It would be nice. Lakeside with a fire...

Of course, Matt would be there.

I tried not to look at him basically the whole ride out to Bear Lake.

Shae was in the back and she was in charge of the music, and so far, the whole ride had been somber and quiet.

So maybe Matt wasn't as unaffected? Maybe?

The question was, did I want him to be?

Thinking about that moment between us made me have to cross my legs. I squirmed in my seat and my eyes were drawn to his hands on the steering wheel. I remembered what they felt like burning through my clothes as he held me.

I wished I could remember what that press of my lips to his had felt like. I couldn't actually believe I'd done it. The act seemed to have been like lighting the fuse on a stick of dynamite.

And it was still burning.

I guess all I could do was wait for the inevitable explosion?

"You guys are so quiet. What's up?" Shae finally demanded.

"Just thinking," I said.

"About Rathboner?" Shae teased.

"Maybe. Maybe not."

"So tell me. Is the hype all true?" She leaned forward into the space between the front and back.

"I don't know. I didn't do it yet."

"Hmm."

"Why hmmm?" I asked.

"I thought you wanted to get it over with?" Shae asked.

"I did. But I mean, you can't just..."

She laughed. "You can just."

"He offered to just."

"Can we stop with the justs?" Matt said. "Call it what it is. *Fucking.*"

"I'll call it what I want." I narrowed my eyes at him.

"For fuck's sake. Literally," he said.

"Damn, Matt. You're like a growly bear. What's your damage?"

"Nothing," he said. "Just ready to unwind a bit."

"I thought we weren't justing?" I teased.

He smiled at me.

His face was so familiar, so dear, and now, it had become something else. Something I coveted. I wanted to know what it was like to be able to touch him in any way I wanted, any time I wanted.

I desperately wanted to know what it was like to really kiss him. To have him look at me like he had the other night all the time.

Then Shae did us all a favor and put on a bop. We were all singing along when we finally arrived.

I had to put some distance between me and the Matt situation.

Because the thing was, even if something happened between us, I still wanted to experience Sebastian.

God, maybe I was making up for my years of celibacy by just throwing myself on my back and telling them all to line up and take a number.

It was complicated.

After we picked rooms, that we all knew we probably wouldn't actually be sleeping in, we went outside to the bonfire and I went ahead and made my way down to the lake.

I wandered around until I found a beachy area away from the dock and I sat down and put my feet in the water.

I knew I needed to make a decision about Matt. About Bastian.

About me.

I needed to choose what I wanted, what I could accept, and acceptable fallout.

I don't know how long I sat there, digging my toes into the sand and letting the water lap at my ankles while I looked up at the clouds as they passed.

After a while, a shadow blocked out the sun.

"You ran away awfully fast, pretty Jax," Sebastian said.

"I suppose I did."

"Is there something wrong?" He sat down next to me and leaned back. "Have you changed your mind?"

"No. I don't think so."

"But?" he prompted.

"You know, for all that you act like you're just some kind of playboy, I can see that your well runs deeper. A lot deeper. You see people and I think you want to be seen."

"Don't... you know what? Maybe I will tell you. Maybe I should."

"I think you should tell me whatever you want to tell me. I thought I didn't want us to be friends, but I do like you, Bastian."

"I think one should generally like the person they first have sex with, but I've been told by our illustrious Shae I'm no expert."

"Shae does know a lot of things." I nodded, but I grinned. "You can tell me anything. I'll lock it in the vault."

"It's not something I'm hiding really, but I don't call attention to it often, I suppose." He reached out and took my hand.

I locked my fingers tight with his and turned my head so I could look at him.

We, the women of Hollingsworth University, had come to a consensus that Bastian and Huntington Dane were both disaffected playboy fuckboys who had only one set of skills to offer the world. Maybe two, if you counted their money.

Except in that moment, I knew I was wrong.

Bastian was vulnerable. I saw something on his face that I could swear was self-doubt. Maybe a bit of fear.

I squeezed his hand to reassure him. "I know you see me. Let me see you."

"Ah, you're determined to get me naked in the way that doesn't involve clothes, aren't you?"

"Only if you want to."

"I guess it's fair. You're giving me a first, maybe I should give you one? I've never told anyone this. I've... I've done things. I've done all the things, really. I know they call me a jaded fuckboy."

I felt guilty now having ever had the thought.

"Yeah, but I mean, that's how you want people to see you."

"You're right."

He squeezed my hand back and we lay there silent for so long, I thought he wasn't going to tell me. Then he spoke. "I'm bisexual. It's why I keep people at a distance. It's easier for women in some aspects. But bisexual people are marginalized by straight people *and* gay people."

"Have you ever told anyone before?"

"Not like this. I had a girlfriend once who at one of these parties dared me to kiss another guy, and I did it. Afterwards, she broke up with me. She said I was disgusting because I liked it. I know that's not true, but..."

"That's awful, Bastian."

"Yeah. So here I am. Naked." He exhaled. "Do you still want to be naked with me?"

"I do," I said. "Kiss me again."

He rolled on top of me, his hair so golden in the sun. Our eyes met and again, the world stopped.

"Still no strings?"

"That would be a lie. We have strings now, Bastian. But they're the friendship kind, don't you think?"

"Friends, you say?" He pretended to look confused. "That'll be new."

It was wild how absolutely uncomplicated my feelings were about Bastian. About what I wanted from him and what we could mean to each other. I liked how simple it was.

And oh my god, it felt so good.

He kissed me slowly, as if I was the only woman in the world. As if we were the only creatures in existence. I ran my hands over his back, his biceps, I took my time exploring his body.

I didn't want to be there in that moment with anyone else.

For a moment, I'd been concerned I'd think of Matt. I'd feel guilty it wasn't Matt, but I didn't. We were only friends.

Of course, Bastian and I had agreed to be friends.

He moved from my mouth to my throat, his hands cupping my breasts, moving down my hips. He didn't rush. He wasn't pulling out a condom as soon as he tugged off my shorts.

He did however stop to lay out his shirt. With a grin, he said, "So neither of us get sand up our asses. That's not a good experience."

I laughed and moved onto his shirt. This was easy with him.

He kissed down between the valley of my breasts and made his way to my cleft, and then he dipped his head.

I'd never done this before. I'd been touched there, but not with someone's tongue.

It was possible I'd died. Nothing could feel this good and be real.

"Do you like this kind of kissing," he said, his fingers doing the work his tongue had been doing.

"Oh god yes."

"Then tell me. You were holding your breath. Don't be afraid to breathe. To speak. To say harder, faster, or softer. Or no."

"Okay. I just didn't want it to stop."

"It won't stop until you say." He dipped his head back down again.

I understood everything now. How and why that girl had sounded like a re-boot of The Exorcist. How I could look anyone in the face after they'd... it was all so easy with Bastian.

I arched my hips up to meet him and he grabbed my ass, using it to hold me where he wanted me. I was digging my fingers into the sand, seeking some kind of purchase to hold me grounded while my body floated away.

I came so hard I saw black stars flashing behind my eyes.

"Do you still want this?" he asked.

"Yes."

I was lost in a haze as he pulled out the condom and finished undressing. I felt drunk in the best way. Waves and waves of pulsating bliss echoed through my body.

Except when he rose above me, I knew a moment of fear.

"Hey, it's okay. We'll go slow." He kissed me again and I started to relax.

It didn't hurt when he was inside me. It was strange, different, a fullness that was a little uncomfortable for only a moment, but no pain.

"That's it," he said. "Fly with me again, Jax."

And I did. I flew so high that I never wanted to come back down.

When it was all over, I lay there next to him wondering if I'd been hit by a bus. The world hadn't changed like I thought it would, but *I* had changed.

I felt different.

New.

Strange.

Yet, still me.

And Bastian was still Bastian.

"Come on, into the water with you," he said.

"I didn't bring a suit."

"Neither did I." He winked at me and picked me up, carrying me into the water.

"Oh my god, don't dunk me, my hair is never going to dry!" I hurried to twist it up on the top of my head, but I knew I was probably out of luck.

"No worries. But so what if it's wet. The rest of you is too."

"You're a white boy with short hair. You have no idea."

He laughed. "Fair enough. Let's talk about me, then. So was it all you thought it was? I like to get a good rating."

"Oh, I'll rate you the highest. Can I tip on the app?"

He laughed. "Yeah. You can totally tip."

"It was really good. I'm glad you said yes." I bit my lip. "I'm also really glad I didn't just go back to your dorm. Or mine. Because then we wouldn't be friends."

"I might like this friends thing."

"Me too."

"You know that Matt's in love with you, right?"

"Shut up. He isn't." That wasn't what I wanted to hear. Mostly, because I'd just managed to stop thinking about him.

"Oh, he is. He just doesn't know it. He hates me so much right now."

"He's going to hate you even more."

"No, I'm pretty sure the hate is at peak fire right now. He walked down the shore a few minutes ago and headed right back when he saw what was happening."

"He saw?" Oh my god. How much had he seen? Had he watched? The idea of that made my interior walls clench with another wave of desire.

And Bastian laughed. "Oh, you like that idea, do you?"

Heat filled my cheeks. "I might."

"It's nothing to be embarrassed about. If you want to give him a show, I'm game."

"What if I said yes?"

"You could just take pity on the man and tell him you love him, too, you know."

"Most definitely not. We're just friends."

"Like you and I are just friends?"

"Definitely not like you and me." I swam over to him and draped my arm around his shoulders.

"Hmm. Maybe the three of us should be friends."

My clit basically exploded at the idea. The thing just incinerated and there was nothing left.

He whispered in my ear, "You should think about that tonight while you're trying to sleep. I know I will be."

"You are hedonist, Bastian."

"I am and you are too. Deep down." He kissed my mouth again. "I should get back."

"Okay. I think I might stay here a little while longer."

"I want to see you again," he said.

"I think I'd like that."

"But don't forget, we owe each other nothing but honesty. If you end up with Matt in your web, don't restrain yourself on my account. In fact, I want you to tell me all about it."

"Maybe you'll be there too," I said.

"Maybe I will."

"I guess it's the same, right? If you're with someone else, you can tell me." I was pleased that the idea didn't bother me. It didn't make me jealous. It turned me on a little bit. I thought everyone should get to experience Bastian Rathbone. It really was a gift. Of course, I'd never tell him that.

"Do you actually want me to tell you about it?"

"I do. It's hot."

"Poor Matt. He's in for quite the ride, isn't he? I don't know that he'll be able to keep up with you. He's so boy next door, apple pie and Chevrolet."

"He is. But you know, not every Chevy is a grocery-getter. He might have a 405 under that hood. We just have to find out." Those were big words for me. Bastian made me bold. I liked that about our time together.

"He just might. I bet he comes back to check on you again. You could ask him then."

"I don't think I'm quite on that level yet."

"See you later." He kissed my cheek and walked out of the water. "I'll leave my shirt here for you to wear back if you want."

I was alone in the cool water and I let myself float. My hair was already wet, so why not indulge?

Bastian was right. It wasn't long before I heard Matt's voice. "Hey, you okay? You've been gone a long time. I was worried about you."

"Come swim."

I half-expected him to decline, but he didn't. He just got naked and strode into the water. Yeah, I'd bet he definitely had a 405.

MATT

I didn't mean to watch them. Not at first.

Until Bastian saw me.

And he didn't stop. He didn't try to hide. Hell, he didn't even break eye contact. He held it.

While he fucked my best friend.

Who I wanted to be fucking.

Jesus Christ. The whole world had gone insane.

I forced myself to turn away, but I'd come back again. I told myself it was just to make sure she was safe, but it was more than that.

I was going to have to tell her because what I'd done was wrong. I'd have to ask her to forgive me and hope that she would. Then maybe things could get back on an even keel. Back to a world that made sense.

Except now, I was naked in the water with her.

She was glowing, beaming. Beautiful. I didn't even care she'd just fucked someone else. My dick was just as hard for her.

"Hey," I said.

"Hey yourself," she answered.

God, what to say?

Well, fucknut. Start with where you fucked up when she told you about the kiss. "So tell me about it."

"Really? You want to know?"

"Of course I do. You're glowing so it must've been everything you wanted."

"It was. It really was." She smiled at me. "You're not... disappointed in me?"

"Hell no. I know I didn't approve of your choice, but you know what's best for you."

"Good. I feel like something changed that was putting distance between us and I don't want that. I can't lose you, Matt."

"You will never lose me. No matter what." I hoped I could keep that promise. I intended to.

"Pinky swear?" She held up her finger.

I linked my pink with hers.

"You're stuck with me until you die, Matt Graham."

"I wouldn't actually have it any other way."

"Even if we get married when we're thirty. There is no divorce. I hope you understand that."

I laughed. "Yeah, I got it." Except I knew it was time to come clean. "I have to tell you something."

"What is it?"

"I came looking for you earlier. I saw you." I couldn't meet her eyes. I was ashamed of what I'd done.

"I know. Bastian told me. But I'm glad you told me too. Why did you watch?"

"I didn't, like, stand there forever or anything. I was just worried about you and then you were... you were this... elemental thing of fire and sex and I couldn't look away."

That was probably the stupidest combination of words that had ever come out of my mouth.

"Oh really? You liked looking at me naked?" she teased.

I realized then she'd already forgiven me.

"You're beautiful. You know that."

Now, she was the one who looked away. "I don't know that, Matt. I'm just Jax."

I wanted to hug her, but decided better not. Since we were naked.

She seemed to know exactly what I was thinking because she said, "Yeah, me too."

We swam for hours. It was like we'd shed all of those new skins that seemed to be tearing us apart. We laughed. We talked. We were just Matt and Jax, together.

As night fell, we finally wandered back up on shore and got dressed. There was no awkwardness, no stolen glances. Everything about our time together had been innocent and pure.

"Stay with me tonight like when we were kids," I said, walking back to the house.

"Okay. Did you bring my shorts?"

"Of course."

By the time we got back to the house, the bonfire had died down and everyone had paired off.

"Does it bother you that Bastian is probably with someone else now?" I couldn't help but ask.

"No." She smiled. "It's all good. We talked about it. I think we're going to be friends."

"I thought you didn't want any strings? Not even friendship?"

"It just happened." She shrugged.

We both showered and got ready for bed. She was on her usual side of the bed when I came out, my hair still wet.

She patted the bed. "Come on. Snuggle me hard."

I held her close and it was a relief to feel the familiar shape of her curled up next to me with no reserve. We were back to us somehow.

Until I awoke some time during the night and I'd become the "little spoon." She was behind me, her arm over my stomach, and her hand was perilously close to my hard, throbbing cock.

That was bad.

So I rolled over. If we were nose to nose, the rest of our bodies wouldn't be touching.

Except she rolled over too and pressed her ass right up against me.

This was officially hell. So I just laid there and waited to die.

"Are you awake?" she whispered softly.

"Yeah."

"This is wrong, right?"

"So wrong."

"Then why does it feel so good?" she asked.

"God, it does. But this isn't what you want, is it?"

"I don't know." Her voice was small, quiet, as if she'd been afraid to answer.

"Then it doesn't matter how good it feels."

"What if I said yes?"

Those words punched me right in the gut. "Then I guess we'd have to talk about it. We should probably still talk about it."

"But we're okay, right?"

"Yeah, we're okay." But were we? I really wanted to hug her, but it wouldn't stop there.

"I wanna be close to you, but we can't now, can we? Things have changed."

"I refuse to let my dick get in the way of our friendship, Jax."

She giggled. "I mean, it is kind of actually in the way."

"Shut up." I laughed.

She rolled over to face me, and I opened my arms, pulling her close. "There. Now be quiet. Quit wiggling and go to sleep."

"Fine."

Except she wiggled some more.

"I think you're just being mean now."

"I'm really not. I can't get close enough to you."

God help me. "We're as close as we can get, baby."

"Are we? I wonder if we tried really hard..."

"Yeah, now you're just pushing that button until you break it."

"Can I break it?"

"I don't know. I guess we'll see. That'd be easier though, wouldn't it? If it would just break and..." I sighed.

She put her hand on my face. "I'm sorry. I'll be still."

We lay there in silence for a long time, and I prayed for dawn. Stupidly, I thought daylight would be some sort of relief for my problem.

But it wasn't.

The next day brought Truth or Dare.

Before I even sat down as we were all getting ready to play, I knew a moment of panic. Something in my head told me to get up and leave before I did something I couldn't come back from.

Except that was the point, wasn't it? Playing these games were about doing things you wouldn't normally do, but maybe wanted to? It was a way of abdicating responsibility.

We all gathered in the front room. It was Me, Shae, Bastian, Lauren, Jax, Huntington Dane and Asher Warren. I didn't know Asher well, but she and Dane seemed to have something going on between them. Everyone else who didn't want to play had gone home, as per the rules of the house party.

"So if you're here, that means you've agreed to play," Barclay Wyndham Scott began. "The rules are as follows. Our games are what I call *mostly*. As in mostly safe and mostly sane. But they're always consensual. If the object of any dare doesn't want to participate, that is their right, but that is not without consequences. You will be removed from play. You may return for future games. No dares with penetration, except mouth to mouth kissing. No incest." He eyed everyone. "You all know Hunt is my brother. Don't make it weird. No bestiality. Etc. and so forth. Things revealed during Truth turns will not leave this cabin. Or you will not be invited to play again. Does everyone understand and agree?"

Everyone nodded.

That feeling in my gut twisted on itself and briefly, I thought about backing out. But looking across the room at Jax, the excitement in her eyes, I couldn't do it. I'd have to play this out to the end no matter what happened.

"If everyone is ready, I'll start," Barclay said. "Bastian. Truth or Dare?"

"Dare, obviously."

"I dare you to give Matt a lap dance," Barclay said.

I thought about what had happened earlier. Watching him with Jax.

"To what song?" Bastian was already standing up.

"*Push It* by Salt N Peppa." Shae was gleeful when she cued up her phone.

Bastian turned toward me, asking for consent, I think. I shrugged.

What else what I going to do? Say no? Not likely. Especially not when I felt Jax's eyes on me. It was a laser-like heat that was a precise weapon.

Bastian didn't hold back. It made me wonder if he'd taken a walk on the stripper side because this man knew how to move his body. He actually climbed up on my lap, and ground his hips against mine. His cock was hard and thick, the way he moved, his hands on me, it made me hard too.

It was unexpected.

But it shouldn't have been. When I thought about him with Jax, I wanted to be part of it too.

That thought surprised me, but it shot stabs of lust through my body hard and fast.

So I didn't hold back either. Not when our eyes met, and I locked my hands onto his hips.

When the song was over, the spell was broken.

Bastian smirked at me, and I didn't know what to do with myself. With the space I occupied.

So I said, "Thanks?"

"Yeah, thanks. For sure." Shae gasped.

"Shit, game over. I don't think any of us can outdo that. Not with our clothes on, anyway," Lauren said.

I sat there in a haze of lust, processing what had just happened. Not only between Bastian and I, but the turn my thoughts had taken. I'd never been attracted to another man before, and if I'd considered it, I would never have expected to be attracted to Rathbone.

But I was.

"Happy to be of service." Bastian winked, but then he turned to Jax. "Jax, Truth or Dare?"

"Truth," she blurted. "Shit, I meant to say dare, but I'm a giant coward."

We all laughed, but I had this sneaking suspicion Bastian was going to ask something to twist things up between the three of us, and I wanted him to.

"No worries. Why did you pick me to pluck your cherry instead of Matt?" Bastian asked, still smirking.

That was not the question I wanted him to ask.

Jax looked terrified. "Jesus. Did you see yourself just now? Of course, I picked you."

"You didn't see that before you chose me," Bastian said.

"And you asked, and I answered." Jax looked away.

"Shae, Truth or Dare?" Jax was quick to change the subject.

I found myself lost in my own world as the game continued. It was a haze of questions with no answers and answers without questions. *Lust. Need. Self-realization.* This was that moment. That thing I knew was going to change irrevocably.

It was both as terrifying as I thought it would be and surprisingly easy to accept.

At least, it was, until Asher yanked me out of my fog by asking, "Matt, truth or dare?"

"Dare." Obviously I would pick dare. I responded before I even had a chance to think about it.

"I dare you to make out with Bastian. I think we all needed a little more of that," Asher said.

I could feel my face burn with a blush. Which was stupid, but I was embarrassed at being dared to do something I wanted to do. Again, the whole point of the game, right?

I licked my lips and went over to Bastian. "This cool?"

Consent, first and always. I knew Barclay said that playing implied consent, but that wasn't good enough for me.

Bastian stood and grinned. He grabbed the back of my neck and slammed his mouth into mine. God, I couldn't stop thinking about his mouth on Jax, and now his mouth was on me.

I gripped his shoulders and pulled him closer, tasting him, enjoying his heat. The contrast of how hard he was. How much our bodies were alike, honed and strong. The way we fit together.

He broke the kiss, and I was drunk on him. On us.

I sat there, dazed until I realized everyone was running down to the lake, stripping off their clothes as they went.

In for a fucking penny, I figured, so I stripped and ran down to the shore to join them.

Everyone was laughing and splashing around. I dunked myself a few times to wash away the heat that still suffused my body and my brain. I swam out to the floating dock and crawled up to lie out in the sun.

I don't know how long I laid there, but my skin was dry when I heard Bastian's voice. "You good?"

"Yeah. Surprised, but good." I really was.

"There is a certain kind of man that wouldn't be, you know. He'd be pissed he got a hard-on with another man. He'd want to make that man pay for making him feel something he thought was wrong." His tone was casual, but his words hit me with a fist.

"What kind of shithead do you think I am, Bastian?"

"I didn't say you were a shithead. I was just protecting myself. I've had experience."

"You don't have to protect yourself from me."

"Good." He climbed up on the dock and lay next to me, his hands behind his head. "We can be friends, right?"

Did I want to be friends with Bastian? I was pretty sure I wanted to fuck him, but could we be friends? Jax seemed to be doing a pretty good job of it.

"Jax recommends your friendship highly. I trust her judgement, so why not?"

"Do you want to talk about what happened on the beach? I mean, since we're all friends now."

"I apologized to Jax. Would you like one, too? I shouldn't have watched."

Bastian laughed. "Oh no, my man. The only thing you did wrong was walking away. You should've joined."

I was rock hard again at his words. God, my dick hurt.

"Yeah," Bastian said. "You definitely should've joined."

Remembering the way we'd kissed, I said, "I didn't know I had an invitation. And I didn't know I wanted to."

"Fair enough. We should hang out sometime, Matt, the two of us. We could see what else you don't know you want."

I was torn. I wanted to, but this thing that was happening between Jax and me...

"Or not," Bastian was quick to add.

"Hey, I... it's complicated."

"It doesn't have to be." Bastian winked at me and dove into the water, swimming farther out.

I swam back to shore and went back to the house. There, I took a shower and beat my dick raw thinking about what it would be like between Jax, Bastian and me.

JAX

I COULDN'T UNSEE what happened between Matt and Bastian.

I didn't want to.

I felt slightly guilty for objectifying him. But only slightly.

On the ride home, Shae asked if Matt could drop me off with her, and I agreed because she looked upset.

After Matt had gone, and we were inside, she said, "I have to tell you something."

From the look on her face, I thought for sure she was going to confess to me that she'd slept with Matt.

Which I couldn't be mad about. He was my friend. Not my boyfriend.

But that wasn't it at all.

"Something happened with Bastian." She rolled her eyes upward, as if a plea to the heavens.

"What happened?" I took her hand and squeezed.

"I'm really sorry, Jax. I feel like an asshole."

"You're not an asshole. Bastian and I aren't dating. We're not together. You didn't do anything wrong."

"Are you sure?" She looked so haunted. "I mean, you chose him to..."

"And he did. It was great, but that's it."

"Really? Oh my god. Tell me about it. Wait, I really hope he wasn't with us the same day, because..."

"Because why? You're my best girlfriend. Why would that be bad?"

Shae stopped. "You know, I didn't think about it that way. I'm supposed to be some kind of sexpert, but I'm feeling a little out of my league here."

I laughed. "What? No. I mean... I've been feeling out of my league for years. Sex is fun. Pleasure between people who care about each other is good, right?"

"If that's the case, why haven't you slept with Matt yet?"

"Shut up."

Shae laughed. "It's nice to know we're both in the deep end."

"Can I tell you something?"

"Anything."

"I'm thinking about sleeping with them both."

"Wow. You went from virgin to sex goddess overnight."

"Yeah, you know me. I don't do anything half-assed. Or half-vagged, apparently."

"That would be so hot, and I'm so jealous," Shae said.

"I don't know that I'm quite ready for four, but the idea is kind of hot?" It was definitely a question.

Shae blushed. "I... yeah. That's hot. I think it's so cool that you're not hung up on any weird ideas about what you should be doing with your body. That you're exploring everything you want to without worrying about what anyone thinks of you."

"Well, I was a virgin up until this weekend. I need to catch up."

"Not with anyone else. I mean..."

"No, no. This isn't a competition with anyone else or with what I think society thinks I should be doing sexually. This is me catching up with my own head. All the things I've thought about and all the things that have turned me on."

"That's hot, too."

"Really?"

"Yeah." Shae squeezed my hand again. "So, it's really okay? I mean, I might see him again."

"Bastian and I don't owe each other anything except honesty. Fuck his brains out, with my well wishes." I found I meant it.

There was something between Shae and Bastian, whether either of them wanted to admit it or not. Something that even I could see was more than electric attraction.

"Thanks? I wonder how he'd feel if he knew we were trading him like a baseball card?"

"I think he'd be flattered," I said.

"So, I was thinking of hosting a game here. Spin the Bottle. What do you think?"

"I think it's a good idea. I'll play!"

"Really? I mean, our game of Truth or Dare was so intense. Just a little kissing game, with only kissing, couldn't possibly measure up. Could it?"

"It depends. I think it'll be fun."

"Okay. Let's work on a guest list. Definitely not inviting Hunt."

"Why not? He's such a bastard. He'd make it fun."

"Yeah, but I don't want to have to kiss him. I'd probably like it, and then there'd be no end to my shame."

"That's fair. Asher seemed pretty into him."

"I know. Poor thing. I can see that's going to crash and burn. They've been sworn enemies forever and now... I don't know."

"Maybe like what happened between you and Bastian?"

"No, not exactly."

"Tell me. I'm dying to know."

"Well, he was bragging about his skills as a cunning linguist, and I dared him to prove it. I didn't think he *would*."

"Oh my god."

"I know, right?"

"I hate to tell you this, but I think you should date."

"I think you and Matt should date. So there." She stuck out her tongue.

"Honestly, I think I have feelings for him, but I'm not ready for that. I've always loved him, but I'm not ready to be in love with him. I have a lot more exploring to do."

"Can't you love him and explore together? Because I think you're both interested in exploring Bastian."

"I don't know." I bit my lip. I seemed to be doing that all the time. The fucker was raw. "The idea of that is so hot, but I'm wondering if it's one of those things that's best left to fantasy instead of trying to make it happen."

"Did you see them in the lake after the game? I thought they were going to fuck right there," Shae said.

"That would also have been hot." I sighed. "I think I'm turning into some kind of sex fiend. That's all I can think about. All I *want* to think about."

"I think that's pretty normal. You spent years on lockdown, and now you've let that part of yourself out. She wants to fly before you lock her down again. You'll even out eventually. Or not. There's nothing wrong with being sex motivated."

"You don't think so?"

"Well, I'm a psych major, so you'll just have to trust me on that. You'll notice I said this in my most professional tone."

I laughed. "I guess I have to take it as gospel."

"You do. You do."

"Okay, so guest list?"

"You, Bastian, Matt. Lauren, Barclay. Maybe Brooklyn. We need another girl."

"Hmm. What about Bonnie? She's adorable. She's a Ridgemont Hall girl."

"Okay, you invite her?" Shae delegated.

"Sure. There, party planned!"

"Oh wait, I think Lauren and Barclay are playing another round of TorD at the Hall. Shit."

"You could invite Brad Barnes and I guess that Winter chick. I don't know that she'd come, but she looks interesting."

"She does, doesn't she? She's extra goth with death sprinkles, but she carries an Hermes bag. I think we need to know her."

"You invite her," I said.

"Fine." Shae grinned. "You know what else is great about Spin the Bottle? It can't really be manipulated like Truth or Dare. Before TorD, you can make bets and deals and pretty much rig it the way you want. Spin the Bottle is completely reliant on chance. The bottle stops where it stops."

"That's actually kind of terrifying."

"It is, isn't it? That's why I want to play."

"So, when Lauren and Asher were making out during the game, they both seemed like they knew exactly what they were doing."

"They did, didn't they? I thought it was especially sexy because, even though they were doing it on a dare from a guy, they were enjoying each other for the sake of enjoyment rather than putting on a show for the menfolk."

I laughed and bit my lip again. (ouch, damn it.) "Yeah. It wasn't awkward or anything." I coughed. "I don't want to be awkward."

"Jax, are you asking me to kiss you?"

"Maybe? If it's okay? I just... I don't want to look like the stumbling virgin."

"Who cares what anyone thinks?"

"It's not just about how it looks. It's about how it'll feel. To me. To the person I'm kissing. I've only kissed four men. And that's the end of my experience."

"I like how you just assume I know what I'm doing."

"Don't you? If you don't want to, that's okay. Was it weird that I asked?" Oh god, I'd just made a total ass out of myself.

"Not at all. Come here."

Shae drew me in. Her touch was so different than any of the men I had kissed. She tilted my chin up with her fingers and pressed her lips to mine. They were so soft, and so was she. All rounded curves and softness.

I bloomed under her tutelage, my lips parting for her kiss.

It wasn't long until we were both breathless and we broke apart.

"I'd say you're going to do fine," Shae said.

"Thank you."

"Absolutely any time." She grinned at me.

My phone buzzed. It was Matt.

Matt: *Everything okay?*

"Matt wants to know if everything is okay."

Shae giggled. "Tell him how okay it is. Give him something to think about."

Me: *Fine. Fine. Just making out with Shae.*

Matt: *If you don't want to tell me, you don't have to.*

Me: *Seriously. I asked her to kiss me because we're going to play Spin the Bottle next weekend. I wanted practice. Wanna come?*

I thought perhaps maybe I should've phrased it another way. Oh well.

Matt: *I'm not going to take that bait. It's too easy.*

Me: *To play Spin the Bottle or coming?*

Matt: ...

Matt: *You've turned into such a naughty girl.*

Me: *You like it.*

Matt: *More than I should.*

My face suddenly burned hot. I'd just made out with my friend. She was going to have sex with the guy I'd lost my virginity to, and I was cheering her on. Yet, here I was, blushing at a stupid text? *Get it together, Jax.*

Me: *So, you're coming?*

Matt: *Not just yet. But soon.*

I looked up at Shae while I hesitated.

"What?" she asked. "Whatever it is, do it. You want to."

"Oh God, I do. Fuck it." I started typing.

Me: *Really? Thinking about Bastian? Me? Or both?*

Matt: ...

Matt: ...

For a second, I thought I'd pushed things too far. Maybe I had. I wished I could take the words back. What had I done?

Then he answered.

Matt: *You. Bastian. Us. You again.*

I pressed my lips together as heat coursed through me, and I couldn't catch my breath.

"What did he say?"

I showed her the text, and she squealed. "Oh shit."

"Yeah. I think there was a line there, but it's so far gone."

"It's already been crossed, so you can't uncross it. All you can do is move forward."

I didn't want to break whatever spell we were both under, but I didn't want to break us, either. Part of me was so tempted to type that I was coming over, but I didn't.

Me: *Who's the naughty one now?*

Matt: *Still you.*

Me: *Nuh-uh. I'm not the one taking advantage of myself. Lolol.*

Matt: *Too bad. You should. Then tell me about it.*

My eyes went wide because I found I wanted to do just that.

"I'm going to die. Death by arousal. Is that a thing that can happen?" I asked Shae.

"I think, after the next party, we're all going to find out."

Matt: *Of course, you'll have to look me in the face afterward. So, maybe not.*

He referred to my giant fear of how I would look anyone in the face after being intimate with them.

Me: *You'd have to look me in the face, too, stud.*

Matt: *Not a problem. Wait, I'm a liar. I'd be looking at your breasts, because I'm always trying not to these days.*

Me: *You can look. What was it you said? What's a little fantasy between friends?*

Matt: *You want me to die, right? You're trying to kill me.*

I ran to Shae's bathroom and snapped a pic of me in my pink lace bra with a smile on my face. Before I could change my mind, I sent it to him.

Matt: *I don't know whether to damn you or thank you.*

Me: *I would appreciate a thank you. And maybe tell me I'm pretty. It's the least you can do.*

Matt: *You're beautiful. Another.*

Me: *Greedy.*

Matt: *You know this about me.*

I took off my bra, stripped naked, and sent him a nude. Again, I'm sure it was a shitty picture. I'm sure I shouldn't have done it. But, in the moment, I wanted to. I liked how this made me feel. I was greedy, too. I wanted more.

Matt: *Jesus Christ.*

I remembered what he said about me calling him god, and how he didn't even have to touch me.

Me: *What was that about calling out the name of god? And I didn't even touch you?*

Matt: *You win.*

Me: *I'm never going to let you forget you said that.*

Matt: *The next round, you're going down.*

I laughed.

Me: *No, you.*

Matt: *Any time you want, sweetheart.*

I gulped. Got dressed again and emerged from the bathroom.

"I trust that went well?" Shae asked.

"Well, we've negotiated oral sex."

Her eyes widened. "Him or you?"

I showed her the phone. She started laughing so hard, I thought she was going to cry.

"Now, I have to look at him. In the face. I don't think I can."

"What? Why is that a problem? You look at Bastian fine."

"I... I don't know. It just is a thing."

"You best get over that. Of course, if he goes down, you don't actually have to look at him."

She had a point there.

But seriously, what had I done?

MATT

Now I was the one with the problem when it came to looking someone in the face. Since Jax had sent me nudes, I didn't think I could face her.

No, it wasn't about facing her.

It was about facing what had changed between us, and I didn't think either one of us was ready for that.

Our text convo had been on fire.

I actually thought I'd hallucinated the nude she sent me, and I kept looking at it. Every time I pulled it up, that playful smile on her face reminded me it was so real.

I also wondered—if it had been me instead of Bastian who'd been her first—if she'd have felt like she could explore like this. Or if she'd have felt locked down.

It might've fractured us instead, honestly.

If something happened between us now, it would be different. Of course, there was still a chance it would do harm, but not like it would've otherwise. I understood that now. I don't think I'd ever have had a chance to explore these feelings with Bastian, either. It would've just been a thing that happened at college, and I wouldn't be about to knock the door of his dorm pod.

He'd said we should hang out some time. I was taking him at his word.

Not that we had any plans. Every time I tried to text him, I didn't know what to say. I didn't exactly have any idea what I was going to say in person, either, but I figured that would take care of itself. I knocked, anyway.

He opened the door shirtless and covered in sweat. His hair was slicked back, and his skin was flushed from exertion.

Fuck me, but what would it be like to have all of that energy focused on you? My mouth went dry.

"Sorry, should've texted," I mumbled.

He held the door wider. "Nah. It's fine. I was just getting a quick workout. Planking until I die. Come in."

I stepped inside his incredibly bare dorm pod.

"Where are your roommates?"

"I don't have any."

"How pissed is Dane that you got a pod all to yourself and he didn't?"

He shrugged. "He could've had it, but he'd already agreed to room with Pandy and Conrad."

"Must be nice."

"It is, somewhat. I've been told I'm missing out on some great experience by not having roommates. I don't know that I agree."

I thought of my own roommates who I didn't see very often, and I couldn't actually remember their names. "No, probably not. I don't see mine, like, ever. We all prefer it that way. It's not that we dislike each other; we're just busy."

"Hey, I was just gonna hop in the shower. You want a beer or something?" Bastian asked.

I would not think about him in the shower. More importantly, I would not think about joining him in the shower.

Well, maybe I would.

"Yeah, sure. Like I said, if you're busy..." I shrugged.

Sebastian studied me hard. Or maybe I was just more aware of his scrutiny, felt it more intensely, because I wanted to hide my thoughts from him and from myself. Not because I was ashamed of wanting him, but because it occurred to me I wasn't treating him like a person. I'd objectified him, as well as Jax.

That's not who I wanted to be.

Sebastian added, "You can join me, if you're so inclined."

I noticed the change in him. He'd been relaxed and chill when he'd invited me inside. A quieter version of the Bastian I knew. Probably the real Bastian. Now, he was *on*. His speech patterns changed, the way he held his body... He'd become the playboy fuckdoll everyone thought he was.

The one people dressed up in their fantasies, and he made like he was happy to play.

Including me.

"I want to."

"But?" he prompted.

"But not if all I get is off."

He raised a brow. "Isn't that why you're here?"

I closed my eyes. "Yes and no. I want to know you. Not the plastic face you show everyone else, but I want to really know you."

"That's the worst idea I've ever heard." He was trying to act disaffected. Somehow it seemed my words really did hurt him.

Fuck. That's not what I was trying to do.

"Bastian—"

"What you want," he sneered at me, "is to not feel bad for fucking another man. You think if you get to know me, if you get to peer at my sticky dark insides, that it'll make it better that you're not the All-American White Protestant Boy Next Door?"

"I'm an atheist," I mumbled.

He narrowed his eyes further. "I don't do feelings."

"No one asked you to. You said at the lake that you wanted to be friends. And aren't you and Jax friends?"

"The way you and Jax are friends." He smirked.

"No. *No one* is friends with Jax the way I am."

"For fuck's sake, why don't you two stop dicking around and just be in love, already? You're being stupid."

"No. I don't think we're being stupid. We both have parts of ourselves to explore first." We weren't being stupid. Right?

"That's what I am. I'm the experiment. I'm the phase. So, why would I give a piece of myself to you?"

"I can understand why you feel that way." I scrubbed a hand over my face. "You're right. I came here because I want to know what it's like with you. Not just with another man, but *you*."

"Oh, there's another trope. You're not gay, just gay for me." He rolled his eyes.

"I don't know. Maybe? I've never felt this for another man. Not ever. Maybe I won't ever again, but maybe I will. Why should I limit my experiences or desires because other people have had the same desires? Or because I might want something else in the future? Didn't you have the opportunity to find out who you are? Why shouldn't I?"

"Because it's so goddamn easy for you." His words were quiet, but the way he held himself, he more naked than he'd ever been. This was a confession. And maybe it was penance too.

"No, it's really not. Honestly, I was thinking the same thing about you. It seems like you're so comfortable in your own skin, but you're not, are you? Is that what you didn't want me to see?"

"Fuck you, Matt. Get out." His face was a stone mask.

This had not gone in any way like I'd imagined or wanted.

"Bastian—" I'd started talking before I figured out what I wanted to say, so I had nothing but his name. Which was just as well.

"Just go."

"Yeah, okay. I really do want to be your friend. If you need a friend, call me." I turned to leave.

"I don't do strings."

"Yeah, just friendship. No strings." I held my hands up.

"You fucker," he murmured with no real heat.

Suddenly his arms wrapped around my waist, and his hot body pressed up against me from behind. His warm breath puffed against my neck. I leaned back against him, and his hands started moving across my abs. Oh-so-slowly did he work his way down.

"Do you think that you'll still want to be my friend after I make you come?"

His words shot white hot stabs of lust through me, and my cock jerked, begging for attention.

"Yes, Bastian. I'll be your friend no matter what happens here."

"Part of me wants to make you prove it."

"I will."

"So, how should I test you?" One hand ventured lower, his fingers delving past the waistline of my basketball shorts. "By making you come or turning you away?"

"Either." I didn't mean it, though. "Fuck it. That's a lie."

"I knew it was."

I turned in his arms to face him. His eyes were dark, like... I didn't have the words to describe them. Stormy? I don't know. But it evoked a similar reaction inside me. Everything was unsteady and on fire.

"How about I make *you* come, and then you can decide how you want to test me?" I didn't let him answer.

I kissed him.

His mouth was hot, and his hands were in my hair. He was still sweaty from his workout, but I didn't mind it because it made his body slick, hot, and hard. I pushed him against the wall, and it seemed he was going to allow me to lead this dance.

I wasn't worried about what I wanted anymore. In that moment, I wanted to make him feel good. *Wanted.*

Beautiful. Just as he was with no artifice.

Pleasure for the sake of pleasure, but...his pleasure.

"You're not going to save me. I know you want to," he whispered against my mouth.

"We all know you always have to save yourself, but I can be your friend," I said as I slid his shorts down off his hips.

"Do friends really suck each other's cocks?"

"Maybe, if they're good friends." I leaned into him and nipped at his throat while I wrapped my hand around his cock. "But since we're not really friends, you'll just have to settle for this." I stroked him.

His head fell back, eyes closed and mouth parted while I watched the waves of pleasure roll over him with every stroke. I liked that I knew just how to touch him. How responsive he was to my every touch and caress.

I felt powerful myself.

His hips thrust forward, and his body tightened as he neared the edge, but it seemed he was determined not to go over it alone.

Bastian's hands were on me, and he matched my rhythm.

It felt so goddamn good.

When we were both on the edge, he wrapped his hand around the back of my neck. We looked into each other's eyes as we fell.

I'd never had such an intense experience.

But I also knew in that moment my feelings for Bastian weren't of the romantic relationship type. Not that I expected they would be, but I'd been open to the possibility.

"So did you get what you came for?" Bastian asked, his breathing still ragged and harsh.

"Yes, and no."

He looked confused. "What? Excuse me?"

I laughed. "I told you. It's not just about...this."

"Oh god, please tell me you don't want to date."

"No. Like I said. We're friends." I grinned at him.

"Fine. Jesus. What is it with you and Jax both?"

"I guess that's just how we're wired."

"When are you both going to figure this thing out? Because you know, it's like watching a soap opera. I don't want to do it, but I can't stop. Now, I'm invested." He picked up his shorts. "And, now, I really am going to take a shower."

"Now, I really will join you."

"I don't recall inviting you this time. See? Boundaries. You start being friends, and then you start sleeping over, and then we'd be in the same position as you and Jax. No thank you."

I couldn't help it. I laughed.

"Fuck it, come on."

We did actually shower. As much as I enjoyed my time with him, I started thinking about Jax.

She was my best friend still, and who else would I tell about what had happened?

Would it change how she looked at me? How she thought of me?

For a single, brief moment, I wondered if it would change how she *felt* about me. Then I remembered that I knew her. I knew her better than anyone else. She'd always love me. No matter what. If she wanted me before I'd had been with Bastian, she'd want me after.

I also realized this must've been what Bastian's whole life had been like. Wondering if he'd be accepted for who he was.

I understood now why he didn't do strings. He cut them before anyone else could.

I wanted to comfort him, to make it better, but I didn't know how.

Or think he'd even appreciate the gesture. No, he wouldn't. Not at all.

"We should do this again some time," I said, before I left.

"Do you really want to, or is that just something you're saying before you leave because you don't know what else to say?"

"Bastian, I do actually have my share of experiences. I'm perfectly capable of saying *thanks for the nice time* and leaving it at that."

"Oh, really? Do you do that often?"

"Actually, not anymore. It was really novel at first, because I was your standard nerd boy in middle school. High school was a little better, but I was always surprised that anyone wanted to sleep with me. Now, I guess I want more than a one night stand." I shrugged.

He studied me more. "You interest me. You're a strange little bug."

"Nah." I almost said that he was the strange one, just as a matter of course, but it definitely wouldn't help the situation. Also, I wouldn't have meant it. I didn't think he was strange at all. "I'm just Matt."

"If we did see each other again, on a friends with benes basis, how do you think that would make pretty little Jax feel?"

I considered. "She and I...we're not..."

"But you *will* be. Come on. We all see where this is headed."

"Maybe. Maybe not." I stopped to think about what Jax would think about the situation, and my dick got hard again. I knew that, when I got old, I'd be sad my dick wouldn't stay hard. Right now, though, I did wish it would lie down and be quiet for about five minutes.

"Oh, is that what Jax would feel, do you think?" He motioned to the tent in my shorts.

"Yeah, actually I do. I think she'd want to try it."

"Try what?"

"Both of us."

He raised a brow. "You think? Here's what I think, because I know you're dying to know. You two will talk all kinds of fantasies, but when you fall into bed with each other, it will be Twue Wuv. Then you'll get married, have two point five kids, a dog and yard. Wait, a summer cottage, too. Once that happens, neither one of you will ever broach the subject of your college indiscretions again."

I considered the possibility, and that actually sounded horrible. "That sounds like a cookie cutter nightmare."

"Doesn't it just?" Bastian said. "A lot of people will settle for it. They'll think love means doing exactly that. After about ten to fifteen years, one or both of them go creeping for the fulfillment they're not getting in the marriage."

"So why stay married? I don't understand that part. If you love someone, why can't you be honest about your needs?"

He shrugged. "But that's how it seems to work in the world, isn't it? Settle for what you think you're supposed to want, and anything that's different, you hide it in the dark."

"I'm going to give you some home truth, since you've had so much to dish up on my plate."

"Oh really? This should be interesting."

"You are in love with Shae."

"No. Definitely not." He looked so offended. As if I'd accused him of putting dog shit in his coffee.

"Yes. You are. You think you can't have her, because you think she wants cookie cutter, two point five, etcetera. But maybe she just wants you."

"No, you've mistaken the part where she likes the way I make her come, much like you, for love. But it's okay, young grasshopper. You'll learn."

"Beware, pride goeth before the fall, my friend."

"Oh, get the fuck out of here." Bastian rolled his eyes.

"We'll see. I'm right."

"So am I," Bastian countered.

"You might be, but not about what you think."

"Are you going to Shae's party?"

"Yeah. You?"

"I don't know. I'm already way past kissing with you, Shae, and Jax, so what's the point?"

"There's a lot to be said for kissing," I said. "Who knows where you'll end up?"

On the way back to my dorm, I realized I'd been talking and thinking about all of these eventuals with Jax, but I'd never really kissed her.

Maybe Bastian was partially right. I'd already laid out my life with her in my head. I'd thought it was normal not to want to think about a life without her, because she was my best friend.

But Jax was always a feature in my future, not an auxiliary piece.

That scared the shit out of me. Neither of us was ready for that.

If we crossed the line too soon…

Just like how she'd known it was best for me not to be her first, maybe now wasn't the time to cross the line.

I didn't know if it would ever be the right time.

I realized I thought of romantic relationships as transient and friendships as the true forever, but where had I learned that? My parents had a great marriage. A lot of people had great marriages.

But there it was. In my head, like a sneaky little worm, was this idea that romantic partners were only temporary.

I had to talk to Jax.

JAX

I WAS SO nervous about the party.

I don't know why. It was just a silly kissing game.

But I knew Matt was going to be there. I hadn't seen him since what I'd come to call The Sexting. I got the idea he was avoiding me.

Shae said I was being silly, except I'd gone from seeing him every day to nothing.

We needed to talk.

No matter how it panned out, I knew it was going to be uncomfortable. Although, I had a feeling I knew how it was going to turn out.

My predictions were that we would talk about everything—we would talk it all to death—then we would decide not to cross the line. Or we would continue crossing the line, whatever. But then we would end up doing it anyway.

An innocent caress, only meant as a casual, platonic affection, would drop a lit match into a keg of gunpowder. We would have amazing sex, then feel guilty about it later.

We would probably stop talking to each other for a while, which would just kill me. Eventually, though, we would come back around, because we don't know how to function without each other. I guessed the only thing still up in the air was how long it would take for us to get to a good place where our friendship was whole and healthy again.

I wouldn't say *back to where we were* because, really, we couldn't ever go back. The same way we couldn't uncross the line.

I thought about the day at the lake when we went swimming together. Our nakedness hadn't mattered then. We'd swam, talked, splashed, and then talked some more.

I wouldn't lie and say that I never thought about what a relationship with him would be like. It'd be just like that, except the naked part would be important, too.

It hit me then, like a brick.

Or maybe it was a wrecking ball.

This was what I wanted. Matt Graham was my forever.

Only I wasn't ready for forever yet. At least, I didn't think so.

Why did this have to be so complicated?

My phone buzzed, startling the hell out of me, and proceeded to do the buzz-ring dance right off my desk. I fumbled and caught it just before it hit the floor.

It was my mother. "Hey, Mama."

"Tell me."

I laughed. My mother always knew when I was feeling something intensely. I was surprised she hadn't called me last week when things had happened with Bastian. I'd actually been putting off talking to her, because I didn't know how to tell her. Or if I was ready to tell her everything.

"You always know, Mama."

"Always. I wanted to call you last week, but I had a feeling I should wait until you called me."

"Yet here we are," I teased.

"If you don't want to talk about whatever it is yet, that's okay. I just needed to hear your voice."

Warmth and calm filled me. The sound of my mother's voice had a singularly magic power to take away all my worries. It was silly, but I even had a video of her on my phone telling me it was going to be fine that I could watch before all of my tests.

"It's good to hear yours, too. How are things going with Robert?"

"He proposed."

I squealed. "When did this happen? What did you say? Of course you said yes. When's the wedding? Am I going to be your Maid of Honor?"

"Whoa, slow down. I didn't say yes. I didn't give him an answer." Mom seemed almost shy about telling me this.

"That's awkward." I didn't want to make any judgements, but how did you go back from being unable to answer a proposal?

"Yes, it is. I told him I'd call him, and it's been three days."

"*Mom.*"

"I know, but I'm not sure it's right."

"You've been dating for three years. I think it's time, to, you know, shit or get off the pot."

"Jacqueline!"

"Well."

"I don't know that I want to be married. I like what we have. I like what I have. I worked hard for my money. For my retirement. For that vacation home I'm about to close on in the Hamptons."

"It's called a pre-nup," I said.

"Yes, he wants one. He has assets, too."

"So what's the problem?" I didn't understand why she couldn't answer him. She loved him. He loved her. Why not get married?

"I don't know, which is why I'm considering breaking up with him. I know you love him, but I don't know if I do." Question answered.

"I love him, but I love you more. I just want you to be happy. So, whatever that is, you should do it. Maybe I can come home next weekend."

"I'm on call every weekend this month and teaching, but we could go to the Bonaire house over Christmas break. You can bring Matt, if you like, unless he's going home with his family."

I straightened my spine and squared my shoulders. I had the idea that, even though my mother wasn't here, she could still see me. Which was creepy if I thought about it too long. "About Matt..."

"Have you two finally decided to get your heads out of your butts and date?"

"I..."

"Oh, please. Of course I know." My mother's tone was pure sarcasm. As if she couldn't believe that I thought this was a surprise.

"Actually, there's more to it." I bit the inside of my cheek. I knew I'd eventually tell my mom about Bastian, but I kind of thought I'd be forty when it happened. Instead, here I was, confessing. Not that she'd think it was a crime, but... "I decided I was ready to lose my virginity."

"Oh. Okay. I trust you made good choices?"

"I don't know if they were the best choices, but they were what I thought was right at the time."

"I'm sure they were. You probably made a list."

I giggled. "Yeah."

"But?" she prompted.

"But it wasn't Matt. He was upset that I didn't ask him, and it's turned into a...a... thing."

"I can see that."

Bless her for not demanding to know how long I'd been in a relationship with the other person or even assuming it was a man. My mother was the best. Although, if I'd gone with the virginity auction, she might have actually killed me.

"He was really nice. I like him a lot."

I didn't know how to say everything else that welled inside me.

She did it for me. "Except you've realized that you're in love with your best friend, but you're not ready to be committed to someone."

"Yes. *That.* I realized that just before you called. It was a relief and a joy to understand my feelings but dealing with the fallout—I don't know, Mama. I just don't know."

"No one ever does. If you're meant to be, he'll understand. And it's Matt. He's always loved you. He always will love you. Don't rush into anything because you're afraid you're going to lose him."

That was how my mother ended up pregnant at sixteen. I'd heard that story.

"It's not just that. My heart hurts. I want these experiences, but I want Matt, too."

"There are all kinds of relationships, little love. Yours doesn't have to fit any parameters except the ones that you define with the people in your relationship."

"You don't think I'm being selfish?"

"No, baby. Not at all. You're being true to yourself, and you can't be true to anyone or anything until you've got that part down."

"I should've just called you to start with."

"Lesson learned." She laughed. "But you'll probably have to learn it a few more times, because I just realized I need to call Grams myself."

"Thanks, Mom." A certain relief flowed through me.

"All this socializing isn't keeping you from the books, right?"

"Of course not." My gaze slid, guilty, to the stack of books in the corner.

"Do you have condoms?"

"*Mom*. Yes. I'm good."

"Just checking."

"I'm going to a party tonight, so I need to get ready. You should call Grams."

"But you're going to study Sunday, right?"

"Yeah. I'll study Sunday."

"I love you. Talk soon."

"Love you, too." I hung up.

I felt better about things, but I didn't know if I'd actually chosen a course of action. Except I knew that Matt and I had to talk.

Really talk and I was going to have to lay everything I was feeling out on the line. I don't know why that scared me so much. Like my mother had said, it was Matt. He was my best friend. I told him everything.

What was there to be scared of? That he didn't feel the same way?

Or maybe that he did?

I got ready and headed over to Shae's.

When she answered the door, her hair was in curlers and her eyeliner had smudged on one eye, making her look like someone had punched her in the face.

"Mistakes were made," she said.

"I can see that."

"No. Not that. I can fix that."

"What can't you fix?" I asked as I went inside.

"This. Tonight. This was a mistake. Why did I think I wanted to do this? Why did I invite Bastian?"

"Because he's fun?"

"Why did he accept my invitation?" she asked.

"Because he's fun." I reiterated.

"He's *not* fun. He's...he's dangerous."

I thought about the way he'd touched me. The way he made me feel. "I guess he might be for some people."

"Fine. He's dangerous for *me*. I can't stop thinking about what happened at Bear Lake."

Me either. Except it wasn't the time with Bastian I kept thinking about. It was Matt.

"Did you tell him that?"

"And become one of his temporary girlfriends? No. I deserve better than that."

I arched a brow, because I had sort of been a temporary girlfriend, but now we were friends.

"That's not what I meant."

"Oh, so you want to be a permanent girlfriend, is what you're saying?"

She growled at me. Actually growled. "No. You know I don't mean that."

"Are you sure? I mean, you're all kinds of a mess because he's coming to this party and..."

"Exactly! I shouldn't be a mess because of anything to do with him. I'm going to call it off."

"Okay. We can tell everyone you're not feeling well. I think I have most everyone else's numbers."

She flopped on the couch. "Except that makes me a giant coward."

"Listen," I told her. "There's a difference between cowardice and self-preservation."

"Except it shouldn't be self-preservation. He's just Sebastian. Rathboner, for fuck's sake." She snorted.

"Okay, so not to poop on your parade, but you know he's more than that. Rathboner, I mean. He's more than a walking life support system for his dick."

"Tell him that."

"I have, in my own way."

"Listen, no. I know you guys have decided you're friends or something, but that's what he puts out to the world. I'm not going to dig deeper or whatever. That's a mistake so many people make. Not believing someone when they show you who they are. Regardless of whether or not it's just a mask, he has a choice in the way he behaves, and that's what he chooses to do. So, no, I'm not going to give him any more credit than 'Rathboner.' He earned the name, and he wears it like a badge, so let him."

"Do you feel better?" I asked her.

"No." She slumped. "Worse, actually."

I sat down next to her. "What are you afraid of?"

She turned to look at me. "The butterflies in my stomach when I hear his name. The way they get drunk when I see his face. How they explode when I think about the way he touched me."

"Agreed. That's terrifying." I nodded.

"I know he doesn't think I'm anything more than a hook up, which is good. Because I couldn't date someone like him. Hell, I don't think I can date anyone. I'm too insecure."

I knew that telling her she had nothing to be insecure about wouldn't help. Not until she discovered her own self-worth all on her own. That didn't make it any easier.

"Does it technically count as a hook up?"

"I don't know. We're both acting like it hasn't happened, and then I got that wild hair up my ass to invite him to this game and, really, why didn't you slap that thought right out of my head?"

"Well, you just said it was up your ass. I mean, you've got a lot going on with stray thoughts in your head, plus self-immolating butterflies in your stomach. I think you're beyond help, my friend. You just have to ride it out. Wait for the butterflies to die, the stray thoughts to wander home, and wild hairs up your ass to... I don't know. Whatever it is that they do."

"You're not actually funny." Shae sighed dramatically.

"Yes, I am."

"Fine. I guess that was a vivid visual."

"Quite."

"What are you going to do if the bottle lands on Matt?"

"I think the question is what I'm going to do if the bottle *doesn't* land on Matt. I think I'd started to believe it would, and I wouldn't have any agency over what happened between us. We could both just throw up our hands and say it's all due to chance. That way, we didn't cross the line."

"Yeah, but you did. You sent him nudes."

"I did. And I haven't seen him since."

"When was the last time you went that long without actually seeing him?" She headed toward the bathroom to fix her raccoon-chic makeup, and I followed.

"Never?"

"Maybe you should talk to him before the game. Or even not play."

"I refuse to be the reason we cancel the game. I'm here to play, whatever happens."

"Are you sure that's what you want to do?" She eyed herself in the mirror, one eyebrow arching in obvious criticism.

Of course I was sure. Wasn't I? "There are more people playing than Matt."

"Exactly. How do you feel about him kissing other people?"

"I guess I assumed I was okay with it." But was I? When he made out with Bastian at Bear Lake, I'd thought it was one of the hottest things I'd ever seen. How would I feel about it if he was kissing Shae?

An immediate white hot stab of jealousy shot through me. What was that?

"Inconvenient, isn't it?" Shae asked, as if she knew exactly what had gone through my head.

"I'll just have to get over it."

"To what end? How long are you and Matt going to do this dance?"

"Until the music stops? Enough about me, though. I'm sure something will play out tonight, and then I'll dominate the conversation with all of my stuff. What about these new feelings for Bastian—"

"They are not *for* him. They're about my interactions with him. There's a difference."

"If that's what helps you sleep at night."

"It does." Shae was grim as she took her eyeliner off, scrubbing at her eye like maybe she was punishing it, too.

"Tell me about it, though. He's really... I know what you said about knowing someone. Believing who they say they are. I swear to you, there's more to him. He's just afraid to show it to anyone."

"But he showed it to you? Maybe *you* should date him."

"What?"

"No, I'm serious. If you're so magical that he can show you his deep dark stuff, why aren't you dating?"

I chose not to take offense at the magical part. I think I might've poked her in a soft place with a sharp thing unwittingly. "Because he didn't have anything to fear by showing me. He knew he wasn't going to lose anything."

"What does he have to lose by showing me he's a person?" Shae turned away from the mirror to look at me.

"I don't know. What do you have to lose by letting him?"

"My self-respect? My pride?" She turned back to the mirror and looked at herself for a long time. "My heart."

"He's risking the same things."

"Goddamn it, I knew you were going to say that." She sighed again. "I'm going to go kick Hunt in the balls."

"Why? What else did he do?"

"He told me at Bear Lake I should hook up with Bastian. That we obviously belonged together. This is all his fault. The maggot that crawled into my brain came from his rotten one."

I couldn't help it. I laughed.

"I'd be rooting for him to get his comeuppance, if it didn't come at Asher's expense. Poor thing is in love with him. I never want to fall in love. I'll fall in lust all day, but I don't want any piece of that."

"You know, maybe you're right."

"About what?" She arched that same critical brow at me again.

"About falling in love. About Bastian. You two could be really bad for each other. One of you is the immovable object and the other is the unstoppable force."

"See? Bad idea all around. The butterflies are just going to have to suffocate. I wish they'd do it soon."

"Maybe some vodka will help."

"Oh, right. I have Wintergreen vodka for everyone. So we'll all taste like breath mints and mouthwash. Yet, maybe get slightly buzzed. Good times will be had by all." I suddenly wasn't so sure. My instincts were screaming at me to leave. Kind of like when you see something in the road and you're not sure if you should drive over it or not then it rips out the underside of your car?

Yeah. That.

And, I mean, most of us end up driving over it anyway.

MATT

BROOKLYN WAS TALKING to Jax when I got to the party. He flashed me a grin when I came inside, and he looked so pleased with himself. I knew he liked Jax a lot. They could be good together.

But if I was honest with myself, the idea of them actually dating was like chewing on tinfoil. It hit a place in my jaw that throbbed through my teeth and down my spine.

For no reason.

Brooklyn was really a decent human being. I had no reason to object.

Except that it wasn't me.

When she turned and saw me, I didn't get her normal wide, open smile. Her unabashed enthusiasm to see me. Her smile was small, shy, and spoke of secret things that were only for us.

I had visions of just tossing her over my shoulder, carrying her all the way back to Ridgemont Hall, and exploring every bit of her with my mouth.

Except I just smiled back.

I would've gone over to her, until I realized how absolutely unfair of me that would be. She was talking to Brooklyn. He wanted to date her. He wanted and could give her the things I didn't think either of us were ready for which each other.

I saw some new faces I hadn't seen at other parties, but I knew. Like Brad Barnes. The new goth princess, Winter Kovach. Her dad was some Eastern Bloc mafia guy, or so we'd all heard.

"Ready for the games?" Bastian drawled as he handed me a shot of something that smelled like mint and hangovers.

"I guess. What is this?"

"Foul, but drink it."

I looked at it and figured might as well. I upended the shot and it tasted like mint and hangovers, too.

"That was disgusting."

"Yes, but everyone is doing it, so we'll all taste minty fresh. Just in case someone had garlic, onions and day-old smashed assholes for lunch."

"Yeah, I have to say day-old smashed assholes not on my list."

"Me either, but that little bit might be." Bastian gestured toward the goth princess.

"She might. She looks like she'd rather bite you than kiss you."

"I know. I love it." Bastian grinned. "I was wondering if I'd have to ask nicely to get her to bite me."

"Those waters are too deep for me."

"What are you looking at?" Winter demanded, with her hand on her hip.

"Well, you, of course," Bastian replied.

"What about me?" She crossed her arms over her breasts.

"Well, my friend and I were talking, and he said you'd probably rather bite me than kiss me, so I said *please*." Bastian winked at her.

"I don't like jocks. Or manwhores. I've heard about you, Rathboner."

He put his hand to his heart. "Does that mean, if the bottle puts us together tonight, I won't get to taste those poisonous lips?"

"Maybe. Depends on if you're a good kisser. See, I require the best of everything."

"He's the best," I agreed.

"How would you know?" She arched a brow.

"Because I made out with him during Truth or Dare." I shrugged, as if it were common knowledge and not a big deal.

"That was a dare. I wouldn't call him the best unless you went back for more," Winter said, her voice heavy with sarcasm.

Bastian shrugged, but I decided to confess. "Well, I did." I winked at her. "You two kids have fun."

As I was walking away, I heard her laugh. "Okay, I guess you Ridgemont guys aren't the assholes I've heard you were."

"Oh, we are," I called back over my shoulder. "At least, some of us are."

I saw Shae downing another of those awful mint shots, and she shoved another one at me when I approached.

"No, I'm good."

"Did you have one?"

"Yes. And I'm sorry I did."

"Right, but no one else will be." She downed another one.

"Do you actually like the taste of that, or is there something wrong?" I asked her.

"I can't even. I'm just..."

I took her hands. "Hey, what's going on with you?"

"Nothing." She squeezed my hands and held them for a moment. "I'm fine. Just trying to empty this bottle so we'll have something to spin."

"Oh, really? I'll believe that when shit sticks to the moon and tastes like..." I picked up the bottle. "Wintergreen fucking vodka."

"It might. It just might."

"Well, you know you can talk to me if you need to talk."

"I don't know that. I heard what you said about Bastian."

"Did you? Does it bother you?" I asked her, a sort of sick feeling turning in my stomach.

"Not at all, insofar, as what it is."

"What do you mean?"

"Two hot guys having hot sex? I am *all* for it. But when it comes to Bastian, it's complicated."

"That I understand. It seems like everything's complicated."

"I know! Why can't things be simple?"

"Maybe we won't appreciate it if it's simple. Or maybe we just make everything harder than it has to be."

"Maybe we do. I think everyone I know is just a ball of anxiety, doubt, and insecurities stuffed into a meat sack."

I considered. "Well, basically. Yeah."

She laughed. "I don't know what I'm doing here. I don't think any of us do. It would be helpful if someone downloaded the instructions."

"Yeah. I'll agree with that, too. Remind me sometime, and I'll tell you how much it sucks when no one knows what's going on."

"What do you mean?"

"My first time? Yeah. Neither of us knew what to do and it was bad. All that stuff about just trying to make each other feel good, and you'll figure it out? No. I needed a diagram."

"Porn?"

"Not helpful."

She laughed again.

"Glad my pain and suffering amuses you." Except I grinned at her.

"You knew it would. For your next story, I want to hear about how you and the love of your life had your first real kiss in my apartment playing Spin the Bottle."

"It's up to fate, I guess."

"It doesn't have to be. It can be up to you."

"If it's up to me, it's not going to happen."

Shae quirked a brow. "I don't understand. I know she sent you nudes. You're best friends. What's not to...?" She held up her hands in a helpless gesture.

"We're best friends. Neither of us are ready for a forever commitment yet, and that's what it would be. Until curiosity or immaturity or any other number of things would pull us apart."

"That's what your mouth says, but if that's such a concern for both of you, why are you here? Willing to risk chance? Because you both want it." She held up her hands. "Even against your better judgement."

"That makes it worse."

"I guess we'll see what fate has to say. Although, if the bottle doesn't land on her, you should kiss her anyway."

"Yeah, like that would happen naturally. 'Hey, come in Shae's bedroom so we can talk...'" I snorted.

"If that's what it takes. There's condoms in the side table."

"For fuck's sake."

"Yes. For fuck's sake. And everyone else's around you. We're all invested and dying to see this come to fruition."

"No one said you perverts get to watch."

Shae eyed me and looked pointedly at Bastian. "Or join?"

I coughed and downed another shot of the mint death, scowling the whole time. "Fine. Are we going to start this shitshow, or what?"

"Yes, we are. I think we should do it right here on the island. We can use this as the tabletop, and everyone is already standing, so it won't be this awkward get up and sit down sort of thing. Or trying to lean across the bottle and knocking everyone's drinks over."

"Seems legit."

"Are you just agreeing with me or really?"

"Really. Listen, even though it's probably better for my health, I never just agree with Jax. So if I don't do it for her, I'm not doing it for anyone else."

"Yes, you do." She snorted.

"Well, sometimes. But only if the point is to make her happy."

"You're both so adorkable, it's disgusting."

"Hey, I come from a long heritage of dorkdom." I wasn't ashamed to admit it.

"You?"

"Yeah, me. What?"

"But you're a jock." Shae looked doubtful.

"Yeah, that's a recent development. My body had to catch up with my head." I shrugged. "I used to look like a pelican. In head gear. Once it did, though..."

She laughed again. "A pelican? No, I'm sure you didn't."

"Dude, this nose?" I tapped the bridge of my nose. "It was a beak. My head was so big and the rest of my body was just kind of this stick."

"Well, we all have an awkward phase."

"My dad still looks like a pelican. Good guy, but total pelican."

She snorted. "Okay, mission accomplished. I'm not upset anymore."

I hugged her. "Good. This was a fine plan. We're all going to have fun."

"Even with all the drama that's sure to happen later?"

"Like Hunt said, isn't that why we play?"

I could feel Jax's eyes on me, and when I looked up she was with Brooklyn, but her eyes were unreadable.

That was new, and I didn't like it. I always knew what she was thinking. Or, at least, I thought I did.

I winked at her.

She raised her left brow, and her lips pursed.

I grinned.

She flashed me the full wattage of her real smile, and I'd never been so happy to see it. No matter what happened, we were going to be okay.

I mean, I knew that, on some base level, but it was nice to have confirmation.

I should've talked to her before today. I should've done more than text.

"Okay, guys. This is my first hostess gig," Shae began.

Everyone quieted and gave her their attention.

"I haven't hosted a game before, and I know some of you haven't played before, so I'm going to go over the rules. Our friend Barclay says that these games are what he calls *mostly*. Mostly safe, sane and consensual. By agreeing to play, you're consenting. Of course, if there's anyone you don't want to interact with, you're free to pass." She coughed. "But that will mean you will be excluded from the next round of games, because we only want to invite people who will play. I don't know if you've played Spin the Bottle before, but this is how we're going to play. When the bottle stops spinning, the person the front end of the bottle points at and the person the back end of the bottle points at will kiss. After everyone has had one kiss, parties are free to retire to other rooms. As this is not our parents' house, I've cleaned out two closets, the pantry and the laundry room." She grinned. "Also, what happens in the game stays in the game. If you're caught spreading rumors, you won't be invited to play again, and there will be other more serious social consequences."

I wondered if she knew that her place was kind of a big deal, considering she was a college student, too. My parents did okay, but I still had loans I'd be paying off until I was old.

"Who is going to do the spinning?" Winter asked.

"The person the front end of the bottle points to. But to start, you can throw the starting pitch."

"I didn't sign up for that."

"Yes, you did." Shae grinned at her. "Come on. Let's play!"

Everyone gathered around the island and Jax squeezed in right next to me. Disappointment crashed in my gut briefly. It couldn't land on her if she was next to me. Maybe that was the point. We didn't need to have that conversation at all, because she'd made herself clear.

Except she leaned into me and whispered, "You didn't hug me, fucker. You're in trouble."

"I'm sorry. I so solemnly swear to hug the shit out of you after the game."

"Who says I'll let you? My hugs aren't always for the taking. You shouldn't take them for granted."

"Mine are. You can have one any time you want. Whenever you want."

"I'm still mad at you," she said, but her voice held no heat. She wasn't actually mad at me.

"You'll think of some way to punish me, and I'll beg your forgiveness, and you'll love me again."

"Hey, fuckos. You wanna play or just go ahead and get started by yourselves?" Winter demanded.

Jax coughed. "Sorry. Carry on, Mistress of Death."

"I will. Thank you." Winter eyed us both and then spun the bottle.

The first couple it connected was Winter herself and Brad Barnes.

"Oh, for fuck's sake." She rolled her eyes. "So what happens if I don't kiss Preppy McJockface?"

"Nothing," Shae said. "You just go home. No harm, no foul."

"Fine. Come here," she said.

"Hey, who says I want to kiss you, Morticia?" Brad said.

"You know you do. Preppy boys like goth girls. We're like catnip. You're scared of us, but you like it."

Bastian nodded. "It's true."

"That one I like. You..." she shrugged.

"Are you going to keep talking or are you going to kiss me?" Brad asked.

"You come here."

"No. You come over here. You're the one who doesn't want to kiss me. So you make the walk to prove that you're doing this of your own free will."

"This is the dumbest thing." Winter rolled her eyes, but she walked over to him. "Jesus, you're tall." She had to stand on her tiptoes, even though she was wearing some seriously high heels. "Can you help me and participate?"

"Just making sure you're still into it."

She grumbled, but he leaned down. When their lips met, it was some kind of insanity. He moved to pull her closer, but somehow ended up lifting her. She wrapped her legs around his waist, and when they finally broke apart, her dark lipstick was smeared all over his face.

They both looked stunned.

She found her voice first. "There."

Brad didn't say anything, and Bastian handed him a makeup wipe that Shae had so generously laid out on the table.

"No matter how hard you scrub, you won't be able to wipe my kiss off, Jockface."

"Wasn't trying, witch." Even though he scrubbed off her lipstick.

"Your turn, though," Brooklyn prompted and Brad spun the bottle.

The next couple was me and Bonnie. I couldn't remember her last name, but she was new Ridgemont and our group of friends.

She blushed and approached me carefully. "I have to tell you something."

I bent down, so she could whisper in my ear. "My best friend's older brother basically made sure I never got to kiss anyone in high school. So..."

I leaned back and smiled at her. "Understood."

I guided her against me with a slow hand, and when I bent to kiss her, it was a gentle brushing of lips. She melted under me, opening and exploring. When it was over, she said, "Thanks."

"Aww. Why didn't you kiss me sweet like that, Matt?" Bastian asked.

"You want me to?" I asked him.

"Hell no," he answered me. "You're no fun now that I can't push your buttons." He coughed. "At least those buttons. There are others I can push."

"Is it hot in here, or is it me?" Shae said, fanning herself.

It was Bonnie's turn to spin, and it landed on Brooklyn and Brad.

"I'm out," Brooklyn said. "No offense, but I just can't."

Brad shrugged.

"Okay. No harm, no foul, but you know the rules." Shae said.

"I can't stay and just watch? Or wait for it to be over?" Brooklyn said.

"Nope. The rules. If you're not playing, you're not staying. If you need a ride, I'll call you an Uber or something."

"No, I'm good." Brooklyn looked lost for a moment. I knew he wanted to ask Jax for her number. I could tell from the way he looked at her. Instead, he just headed for the door.

"One player down." Shae shook her head. "I know it's harsh but, those are the rules. Brad, you can spin."

Brad spun and it landed on Bonnie and Shae.

Bonnie bit her lip and kissed Shae the same way I had kissed Bonnie. Using what she'd learned.

Then it was Shae's turn to spin. Fate decided she and Bastian would kiss.

"I..." For a moment, I thought she was going to quit playing, but Bastian took her hand.

"The kiss I have to give you, we're not doing out here." He pulled her toward the bedroom.

"The party..."

"It's your kiss." He looked at everyone. "Carry on, kids. Your hostess will be back later."

"Not everyone had a turn yet..." Shae said.

"We're good," Jax said. "I've got this. And uh, you've got that. Go."

"So who is going to spin?" Winter drawled.

"Me." Jax spun the bottle, and it landed on Winter and Brad again. "Fate has spoken."

"Fine." Winter grabbed Brad's hand and looked around the room. "Where's the stupid pantry?"

Jax and I both pointed, and Winter dragged him off.

Bonnie, Jax and I looked at each other and grinned.

"That went much more quickly than I was thinking it would," Bonnie said. "And um, thanks for that." She touched her fingers to her lips. "Definitely thank you."

"No problem," I said.

"I think I'm going to go home. I've had the experience I came to have," Bonnie replied.

"Do you need a ride or anything?" Jax asked.

"No. I'm fine. I'll see you next game, maybe?"

"Maybe," I said.

When she was gone, it was just me and Jax. With the bottle between us.

I thought about what Shae had said. How I could just kiss her now because I wanted to. Because she wanted me to. Or I could leave it to chance.

"Do you still want to play?" I asked her.

JAX

Did I want to play?

What did I actually want?

I looked up at him, at his face so familiar and so dear. It was a face I loved, but it was also a face made of hard angles and a hard mouth I'd dreamed about having on my own.

We should talk before we flung ourselves any farther over the line.

Except talking was hard. Kissing was not.

"Spin," I said.

He laughed and, god, I loved the sound of it. The way he laughed was like home.

Matt spun the bottle and surprise, and it didn't land on either of us. "Do you think it's a sign?" he asked.

It probably was, but I wasn't listening. Instead, I said, "So those pictures I sent you? I took them in that bathroom." I pointed to the door.

"Did you?" His eyes had darkened, his pupil's wide, like an endless pool. He'd never looked at me like that before.

It thrilled me.

It scared me.

It made me wonder how far and how hard I'd have to push to see more that he'd never shown me. What would it take to get all of him?

"Why don't you show me?" he said, his voice was thick and low.

It reverberated all the way down into my belly and between my thighs. I took his hand and led him toward the bathroom.

When he locked the door behind us, I knew another wave of dark thrills as they washed over me.

It seemed so forbidden, so wrong, but so right.

The space had seemed huge before. I'd been so jealous of the roman style bath, the dual vanity sink... it had seemed as big as my room in the pod at Ridgemont. Only now, with Matt here with me, there wasn't enough air. There wasn't enough anything.

It was only Matt, and he'd become this creature I hadn't met before. His presence was heavy, his body so big, and animal fire lit his eyes.

God, I was literally going to die.

He stepped toward me, and I giggled, but his hand cupped my cheek.

"What's funny, Jacqueline?"

Oh, he'd used my full name. Fucker. It made a shiver tingle down my back. "Nothing. I just..." I couldn't catch my breath. I kind of didn't want to.

"I've thought about being in here with you. All the things I'd do to you if I got you alone in this room." He leaned forward, his breath on my cheek. "And I've never even kissed you."

"Do you want to kiss me?" I sounded so breathy and tinny. I wrapped my arms around his neck.

Oh god, this was going to happen.

"More than anything." His lips were on my cheek in the most chaste of kisses, which of course cranked my lust up so high I thought it was going to kill me. It was as if every breath we took was in unison, gravid with the possibility of pure pleasure. "You know what else I wanted?"

"What?" I rubbed my cheek against his and pressed myself as close to him as I could get.

"I wanted to fuck you against that wall."

"Yes," I said.

"Yet we still haven't kissed. You don't know if you'll like the way I kiss you. The way I touch you. You can't say yes."

"Oh yes, I can. I do."

"Except, then I thought, I don't want to kiss you because of a kissing game."

"So kiss me because you want to kiss me."

He pulled back and looked down at me, that intense fire still burning in his eyes.

"Kiss me because you love me. Kiss me because you can't imagine going another minute without kissing me."

And he did.

Then I died.

I don't know any other way to explain the way his kiss made me feel. His mouth on mine. The exquisite familiarity of him, of knowing him, and yet being touched this way.

Matt lifted me onto the vanity, and I wrapped my legs around his hips. He pushed me back against the mirror, yet he cradled the back of my head with his hand.

I thought about all the nights I'd spent in his bed, all the lazy after-noons together, all the times we could've been doing this. It was my new favorite pastime.

Bastian had been good, that was for sure, but this was something on a completely different level.

Maybe a different planet.

I loved feeling his erection against me. Knowing it was for me. I did that to him.

"Lemme take you home, Jax."

"Yes." I dug my nails into his shoulders.

"No, baby. Not home base. Home. Let me take you back my room. Spend the night with me."

Then we'd have to talk.

If it happened here, it was... I guess neither of us would have to carry any blame. We could call it the heat of the moment and walk away unscathed.

Going to his room, that was different. We didn't have to see Shae's bathroom all the time.

His room would be his room for...

"Yes," I said. For better or worse, *yes*.

"Good. For a second I thought you'd changed your mind, and it might've killed me."

"Me, too. Let's go."

He took my hand, as he'd done countless times before, but this time it sent shivers of anticipation through me. I followed him down to his car. When he opened the door for me, the haze of lust fell off like a discarded blanket.

That's not to say him being polite made me not want him. It just reminded me of who we were to each other. What this meant for us.

So, when he got in the car, I leaned over and kissed him again.

I kissed him because I didn't know how long I'd be able to kiss him whenever I wanted to. I kissed him because I didn't want him to have the same realization and change his mind. I kissed him because he was so damn good at it.

"Jax, it's really important to me that we make it back to the dorm."

"Mm-hmm." I kissed him some more and thought about climbing into the backseat. But he'd said that the dorm was important, so I pulled back and licked my lips.

I was glad neither of us tasted like mint anymore. We only tasted like each other.

I had to cross my legs, I was so wet.

It was both terrifying and a relief that the Hall wasn't too far away. We rode in silence, but with his right hand clasped in my left. It was like we were holding on to each other for dear life. As if one or both of us was going to float away.

The dorms were surprisingly quiet, and no one we knew milled around or hung out talking, which was a gift. I hadn't thought about how we'd deal with that. *Great talking to you, but I have to go bang the hell out of my best friend. Catch you later. Love you, miss you, bye...*

Or maybe we would sit there talking until we both realized what a shit of an idea that was?

He unlocked the door to his pod, and we beelined for his

room. When he closed the door behind him, and yet again the sound of the lock clicking into place echoed, I couldn't help but giggle.

"Why do you giggle every time I do that?"

"I don't know. It's slightly intimidating." At the look on his face, I rushed to add, "In a good way."

"Oh really? Do you have fantasies of being locked away and... what's the word, ravished?"

"Shut up. You're never going to let me forget about that romance novel I made you read when we were fourteen."

"Never." He closed the distance between us. "Is that what you want?"

My mouth went dry. "I don't know."

"How about I kiss you again?"

I nodded. "I like that part."

"Yeah? Then why are you still backing away from me? You want me to chase you?"

Shit. We were going to talk. I didn't want to talk, but apparently my stupid body wouldn't obey me. "I'm scared."

"Of me?"

"Of me," I answered.

"We don't have to—"

I swallowed hard. "I think we both know better than that. That we *do* have to."

"Actually, we're free to do whatever we choose."

"Are we? Because I can't walk away. Even though maybe we should. If you don't kiss me again, if you don't touch me..."

"What do you think will happen if I don't?"

"I don't want to find out."

"Hey, so, you have to promise me something," he said.

Stepping forward to meet him halfway, I answered, "What?"

"I like how you didn't say you'd promise me anything."

"That's not who I am. Tell me."

"You have to be able to look me in the face in the morning." He laughed.

"You dick." I was up on my tiptoes, kissing him again.

I didn't know if I could look him in the face after this, but I was going to try. I really liked his face. I didn't want to trade it for his dick.

Except in that moment, I'd have traded most anything for his dick.

"I've been thinking about this for so long, Jax."

His words sent skitters through me and raised gooseflesh on my skin. I needed him naked, because I wanted to do the same thing to him. His mouth was on my throat, his hands under my t-shirt and bra, and somehow, I managed to undress him.

Or maybe I just willed his clothes to disappear, because it seemed to happen like magic. I'd always thought undressing your partner would be awkward and weird. But, like with Bastian, he'd basically done it himself. With Matt, it had just...happened.

I was naked with my best friend.

Matt, who'd I'd known my whole life.

All thoughts of turning back or stopping had fled. *Only forward. Only more.*

His mouth had moved to my throat, and I couldn't get close enough to him. I was dizzy with lust and need, and just when I thought he couldn't push me any higher, he swept me up and carried me to the bed.

Where he knelt between my thighs and kissed me there, too.

It seemed his mouth, his hands, were everywhere at once. I didn't know where I was, when I was, or who I was.

Honestly, it felt like I'd crawled out of my own body and into some dimension made of pleasure.

In a vague, fuzzy part of my mind, it occurred to me that this was highly unfair. I wanted to do to him what he was doing to me. I wanted to tease and taunt his body, to pleasure him, as he was doing to me. Yet, I couldn't bring myself to move. Even if I could've managed that, I wouldn't be able to master the words.

"You taste so good," he murmured.

He unraveled me. Basically, I was a whole person when we started, and now I was just a puddle of nerve endings and ecstasy.

I heard something that sounded like screaming when the orgasm hit, and I realized it was me.

He'd never let me forget that he had me screaming. Once I came back to myself, I'd have to remember to do the same to him.

He kissed me again, and I tasted myself on his lips.

I'd been at his mercy long enough.

"On your back. It's my turn."

A slow smile curved his lips. "Yeah? Far be it from me to argue with a beautiful woman."

I laughed. "Remember that tomorrow."

When he'd complied, I took my time. I explored every inch of him first with my hands, and then my mouth.

I memorized the things that made his body tighten or jerk in response, the way he arched his hips up to my mouth when I used my tongue. I teased and taunted him until I thought he couldn't take anymore—until I couldn't take any more—then I teased him just a bit more.

Finally, I straddled his hips, his cock rubbing just inside of my cleft. When I leaned down to kiss him, a thrust of his hips pushed him inside.

He braced on his forearms and suddenly his arms were around me, his back against the wall and we were moving in unison. My hands were moving through his hair, down his shoulders and his back. His face was buried in my neck.

The angle was intense, intimate. So much more than anything with Bastian. I wanted to feel like this every day for the rest of my life.

Maybe three times a day, if I was being honest.

I was so close to shattering, but I wanted to push him over the edge the same as he'd done to me.

This was one battle I didn't stand a chance of winning.

People talk a lot about flowers in relation to sex. From calling the clitoris a little bud, to deflowering, to...but that's what it was. When I came, it hit me hard, and it was like the unfurling of a flower opening its face to the sun. Each concentric wave of bliss was another petal that dipped through my limbs, as if something coiled tightly in the center of my body had awakened and bloomed.

Stupid, really. Flowery words for something basic, primal and animal.

Yet, there it was.

I knew he felt it too because he said, "Jesus Christ." His voice was harsh, guttural, and his arms had tightened around me like a vice while his hips continued to thrust up, pushing us both over the edge.

After the storm had passed, leaving our skin sweat slicked and my forehead resting against his, I said, "Look, this time it was you who called me God."

"You're not going to let that go, are you?"

"Nope." And the vision changed. That future I'd once imagined of us sitting on a whitewashed porch while our grandchildren played together shifted. Those grandchildren weren't mine and his, separately, playing together as we had when we were children. They were ours. Together. From the children we'd had. From the life we'd built.

My bottom lip quivered because I wanted that future more than anything, but I didn't want it *yet*. My visions of that future started to disintegrate, the edges curling and turning into gray snow like a photograph on fire.

"Hey," he said.

"What?" I knew my voice was shaky.

"Don't leave me."

"I would never."

"No, right now. You were leaving me for whatever 'what if' you were spinning in your own head. Be here with me now. Be present."

"But *what if?*"

"Nope."

I found myself flat on my back, with him above me. In a way, it was like he was sheltering me from the world. The real world. From all the doubts and questions that swirled in my head. From all the scenarios of futures past that bubbled in the shadows of my brain.

I looked up into his eyes, into the face I knew so well.

"I'm not saying it doesn't matter. It does." He put his hand on my face. "But we're already here. Let's stay here a little bit longer together."

"Marooned on Fuck Island?" I snickered.

"Yeah. If you want to call it that."

The warmth I'd seen in his eyes shuttered, which was one of the reasons we had to talk. I'd already hurt him with a casual word. When we'd crossed that line, it had been into a war zone of landmines.

"I..."

"Don't worry about it. It doesn't matter. We'll talk. We'll talk it to fucking death, resurrect it, and talk it to death again. But for now, let me make love to you again."

Making love. Wasn't that what our parents called it? Which was stupid. Sex doesn't equal love. Having sex shouldn't be called making love.

Yet, that's exactly what we'd done, wasn't it? In the heat of everything we'd felt, it had been more than fucking.

Bastian had fucked me.

Matt had loved me.

"You want to again?" I asked. I knew I definitely did. Both to feel that tsunami of sensation again and to avoid talking.

Because he was right.

We would talk it to death.

We'd have to.

"Well, I'm just going to hold you for about ten minutes, and then I'm going make you call me god. Again."

"You're so arrogant. Oh my god."

"See? Did it." He smirked and rolled on his side.

I laughed. "You're lucky I love you."

"Aren't I though?"

My eyes widened.

"What, like I was going to argue with that? I know what's good for me."

"Listen, you can't just agree with me all the time. If I didn't have you to debate with, my skills would get rusty."

"Our to do list is as follows..."

I shivered. "I like it when you think you're in charge."

"I know. So get ready. First on the list. More orgasms."

"How many? I need a definite number."

"As many as I can wring out of your delectable body. Now, be quiet."

"Yes, sir."

He paused and blushed.

"Oh, you like being in charge that much, do you?"

"I didn't realize it until you called me sir. I think we need to explore this," he teased.

"Only if you're ready to get on your knees and call me ma'am."

"I have zero problem with this, ma'am."

"Oh. Well, then." I coughed. "Continue."

"First, let's wring everything we have from this moment. Then pizza. Then we can talk this to death and decide where we want to go. Is the to do list approved?"

"Yes, sir."

He pounced on me, and was ready to go again.

"But, wait, the age-old question," I began.

"I figured you wouldn't be into anal."

"Not that question, jerkface." I sighed. "Pepperoni or cheese?"

"Pepperoni with extra cheese."

"Okay. Carry on. Don't forget my pineapple."

It didn't occur to my lust and bliss fogged brain until much later the next morning that we hadn't used a condom.

MATT

SOMEHOW, I thought that our night together might have exorcised the demons between us. That's what it was, this lust. It was like a demon.

It pounced at the times it seemed we were most vulnerable, raging to roaring life.

Yet, with the morning light streaming on her face, I knew I'd never get enough of her.

I was sure I knew what our talk was going to bring. She wasn't ready for the kind of relationship that we'd have like this.

I knew she loved me. I knew she could see a future with us together. I watched that realization play out across her face last night.

And I loved her.

I was prepared to wait. Looking at her face just like this, yeah. I'd wait as long as she wanted.

Not that I planned on being any kind of a saint, but I'd keep my heart for her. Or rather, she'd keep it, until she was ready.

Her eyes opened slowly, and she rolled over and into my arms. "Don't let it be today yet."

I kissed the top of her head, and her beautifully wild hair smelled like coconut. I inhaled deeply. "Okay, it doesn't have to be Saturday. Since we're marooned on Fuck Island, it can be Friday."

She giggled and burrowed closer. "I'm so glad I have a toothbrush here. My mouth tastes like death."

"Hmm, let's see."

"Oh god, no. We had pizza last night. You're going to have death breath, too."

"Mmm-hmm. Come here. We'll die together."

"No," she squealed.

Of course, she let me kiss her anyway.

"Listen," she said. "We're not going to be those people who poop with the door open."

"If you'll recall, I believe you sent me a snapchat..."

She cackled with unabashed glee. "I did. The lighting was good, and it made my skin look dewy."

"Yeah, but you didn't have to tell me that you were literally..."

"I know. I had to get you back for that time you sent me voice message of you farting the ABCs."

"Ah, intimacy. Isn't it great?" I kissed her again.

"No," she murmured. "You taste like pepperoni."

"You don't want to know what you taste like," I teased.

She gasped, but then narrowed her eyes at me. "You're the one who insisted on kissing me. You deserve what you get. You know what?"

"Wha—?"

She planted a solid kiss square on my mouth and deepened it.

I wasn't fighting her off. In fact, I was ready for anything she wanted to dish out.

"Why aren't you trying to get away? This is gross."

"Is it?"

"No. Not really. But isn't is supposed to be?"

"I don't know. Probably."

"I shall have to think of another way to punish you."

"You could tie me up," I offered.

"But you'd like it."

"Also true."

"I guess we have to talk." She sounded so resigned.

"Yeah, we should, but I'll be honest. I'd rather just stay in that place where it doesn't matter."

"So, what, you think maybe we just shouldn't talk about it? That would mean acting like it never happened. Or god forbid, friends with benefits. I hate that saying, by the way. I mean, the benefits *are* the friendships."

"What do you want, Jax?" I'd thought I wasn't scared of her answer, but I was. I wanted her to say that all she wanted was me. Except that's not who she was, and not what I'd actually want from a partner.

"This, but in like five years?" She stretched out on her back. "I know, it's shitty. It's impossible. It's—"

"Why is it impossible?"

"Isn't it?"

"No. How do you know I don't want the same thing?"

"Do you?"

"Neither one of us is ready for what this is. A relationship? Sure. But *this* relationship? What we have? It's the *one*. You're my one." It was surprisingly easy to confess.

"So what are we going to do?" She grabbed my hand and squeezed it.

"We're going to wait. A year. Three. Five. Until we're both ready."

"What if we fall in love with other people?"

"Maybe we should fall in love with other people so we can learn to love each other better." I swallowed hard. "I know you saw a future with me, and I know it scared you."

"Not because it's you." She bit her lip. "But yeah. Maybe a little because it's you. I don't know why, but when I think forever, I always think you. But when I think forever romantic relationship, I'm terrified."

"Me too."

"Really? I'd kind of hoped you were the one who knew where this ship was going, so we don't sink it."

"Sorry. No such luck."

"We're going to go back to the way we were before? We're going to have platonic sleepovers, and... I just can't see it. I can't see telling you about my latest conquests. Or if I fall in love. Or... I can't. Because I'll see that vision of us old together, and I'll be afraid I'm going to break it."

She was right. "You can't break it."

"But if we can't be friends the same way we were before..." She sighed. "I mean, I already want you to touch me again, Matt. The idea that you're not going to, that we have to stop this—it's awful."

"So maybe we don't stop. Maybe we try this relationship thing, but without traditional boundaries."

"We don't like sharing each other's time already."

"I thought about that. Maybe it would be different this way, because we know it's all temporary."

"This is like having our cake and eating it, too. Which we know never goes well."

"I'm sure we'll have some bumps, but I have faith in you, Jax. I have faith in us. We'll figure it out." But as much as I wanted to believe my own words, I didn't. They rang false in my ears. I did have faith in Jax, I did have faith in us, but I knew it wouldn't be easy.

"What about Bastian?"

"What do you mean?"

"You kissed him. You made out with him. Is that something that you want to explore?"

"I did."

"What?" Her lips parted. "Tell me." Then her eyes narrowed. "Wait, why didn't you already tell me? When did this happen?"

Why hadn't I told her? I didn't know.

"Are you bisexual? Wait, you don't have to tell me. If you're not ready. I'm sorry, it's just, this is a big deal."

"No, it's not. Not really. If I am bisexual, and I might be, I'm only hetero romantic. I liked what happened with Bastian, but I don't have any romantic feelings for him."

"Can I perv just a little bit?"

"I think you already have."

"That's so hot."

"I told him you'd think so."

"You guys talked about me?"

"We did. I told him the three of us together would be really hot."

She looked up at me. "Do you want to do that?"

I knew what she was asking me was *could* I do that. "Yes."

Jax bit her lip and closed her eyes.

"How do you feel about that?"

"Turned on."

"Obviously. I meant, emotionally. Since we're talking about boundaries and what we're doing together."

"Oh. That. Yeah." She sighed. "I don't know."

"Fair enough."

"I wanted to tell you I'm sorry that I hurt your feelings when I didn't pick you. To be first, I mean. But you do understand why, right?"

"Yeah. I didn't at first, but after what happened with Bastian... yeah. And really, you didn't owe me an explanation. It was always your choice."

"We still haven't made any kind of decision beyond that you're going to fuck me again while we both fantasize about a threesome with Sebastian."

It was then that she sat straight up in bed.

"Oh. My. God."

The sheer terror on her face punched me low and hard in my gut.

"What's wrong?"

When she turned to look at me, I saw something worse than her fear. It was betrayal.

"Did you forget something?"

"I...no?"

"Condoms," she hissed.

I could literally feel all the blood in my body drop to my feet and slowly begin to work its way back up to my head. Oh fuck my life. Fuck everything.

"Yeah. Thanks for that." She stumbled out of the bed and began shoving her clothes on.

I was usually so careful. So mindful. I hadn't been thinking.

"I trusted you," she said, her voice shaky. Tears streaked down her face. "I trusted you," she said again.

"Jax, this isn't all on me. You have a responsibility to yourself, too."

"Yeah, you're right. I forgot that with you, because I thought I was safe. Now look where we are. You know why I waited so long. And, Jesus Christ, Matt, I've only been with one other person. *Once*."

I didn't know what to say. I didn't know what to do. "I've been tested."

"Fucking goddamn," she shrieked. "I didn't even think about that. All I can think about is how my mother almost threw her life away for a dick. What if I get pregnant? I told you I didn't want this. I wasn't ready. And you just..." Her hands had curled into fists.

"Morning after pill." I got up and started to dress. "We'll go to the pharmacy—"

"No. *I* will go to the pharmacy. After all, I have a responsibility to myself, don't I?" She was already at the door. "You got something else wrong, too. I *can* look at you. I just don't want to."

She slammed the door.

The place in the bed next to me where she'd laid was still warm. My sheets still smelled like coconut. Her bra was still over the back of my chair. Only I'd never felt farther away from her.

"How could you have been so stupid?" I mumbled.

That little voice in the back of my head kept reminding me that it wasn't just me. We were both at fault here. We both had a responsibility. That it wasn't fair for her to put all of this on only my shoulders.

Yet, she was right. I knew why she'd waited so long. I knew what she was afraid of, and I hadn't considered her. Not really. I'd thought about her pleasure, sure. But I hadn't considered her aftermath. Only the immediate.

I was a better human than that.

Or at least I'd tried to be.

It would figure—the one time, the one place I really failed was when it mattered most.

I wanted to find her and tell her I was sorry, but how did I apologize for that? How did I make it right?

It seemed like a kind of surrender by not going after her. Not making her listen to me. But she said she didn't even want to look at me.

Her words had been designed to hurt, but until she said otherwise, I had to accept that she meant them. I mean, what was I going to do? Go charging into her dorm room and what?

I needed to wait and give her time to breathe.

To think.

To be ready for my apology.

Not that I even knew how to apologize. Not that I was taking all the blame, but I should've immediately owned my part instead of deflecting. That was shitty.

I scrubbed my hand through my hair.

I missed her already. So much. This distance that was between us now wasn't just that she was gone. It was a chasm.

A rift.

This was why best friends didn't make good lovers. The one person I could ask for advice was the one I'd hurt. The one person I went to for solace, for support, for everything except the one thing that had fucked us all up.

And I was late for mandatory gym time. *Shit.*

I hauled ass with both hands over to the gym and got myself on the leg press before Coach realized I wasn't there. I worked my body hard. I kept hoping that I'd hit that Zen place where every other thought in my brain falls away and all that existed in my head was that quiet that happens when I've pushed myself to the limits.

I worked my legs to exhaustion. I could barely stand when I got off the press and then I went to the weights to work my arms. I lifted after gym time was over. I put in every second of my required time and then some.

My arms were about to give out when Bastian pulled me out of my own head.

"Hey, the goal isn't to kill yourself. Let's hit the shower and then the hot tub, yeah?"

"Yeah." I eased the bar back down onto the cradle and my limbs were shaking.

I thought showering with him might be weird, because of what happened between us, but it wasn't. It was just like any other time we'd all hit the showers.

Sinking into the hot tub after the shower was a nice second place to that Zen moment I just couldn't seem to catch.

"So what happened?" Bastian finally asked me.

"Meh."

"Meh? What does that even mean? *Meh?*"

"It means everything's a goddamn mess."

"So you slept with her, right?"

"Yeah."

"And? Christ, I need details." He motioned for me to continue.

"No. You first."

"Meh," Bastian replied. I didn't even have to look at his face to know he was being smug.

"Fine. You're right, it sucks. But I just can't pick this to death right now."

"Maybe neither one of us is too keen on picking open our wounds. What does that leave? Obviously working out your frustration by abusing your body didn't work. What next? You could try to fuck her out of your system, but I don't think that actually ever works."

"Have you tried?"

"Oh, many times."

"Who can't you forget?"

"I thought we agreed, no picking?"

"I don't recall agreeing to that, but we can roll with it." I sighed.

"So listen, I'm new at this friend stuff. What's my job here? Am I supposed to keep asking you or fuck off?"

"That's a complicated question, too. And part of my problem."

"All roads lead to Rome. You might as well tell me."

"I fucked up."

"What did you do?"

I dragged my fingers through the water, debating exactly how much to tell him. I didn't want to dump all of my shit on his shoulders, especially since I knew he was friends with her, too.

"You know I took her home last night. Things... progressed."

"As we all knew they would. Yes. This is the fallout? You just shouldn't have done it?"

"No. There's more. Things were intense. I forgot to suit up."

"Oh shit."

"Yeah. I don't know if Jax told you why she waited until college to have sex, but..."

"She did. I see the problem. She feels betrayed."

"She does, and rightly so."

"Does she own her part in this, too? I mean, neither one of you did that by yourselves."

"I might've suggested that at an inopportune time." I slid farther down in the water. "She's really angry with me. I don't blame her, but I just want to make this better. I already miss her so much. I hate that she's hurting. I hate that I have blame in that."

"Give her some time. I know she'll come back to you. She'll be ready to hear what you have to say once she has some time to think about it."

But what was it I had to say? "How do I apologize for that?"

"I know you think it's complicated, but just say you're sorry. You know you screwed up. And that you love her."

"We haven't even gotten to that part of it. Not really. Before that, she'd said I was what she wanted."

"What's the problem there?"

"In five years."

"Oh. I can see how that would present an issue. God, I really don't want to do this feelings thing. It's messy. It hurts. Why?"

"Did you slip and fall in love?"

"What? No. That would be stupid, wouldn't it? Especially if the person I had feelings for thought I was shit."

"Shae doesn't think you're shit."

"How do you know I mean her? I might mean you."

"Obviously, I don't think you're shit. So, obviously, you don't mean me."

"Ugh. I'm actually sorry that I can't make you blush now. That was fun." Bastian sighed.

"You know, whenever we talk about feelings, you always bring it back to sex. Why do you do that?"

"Oh, are we at this part of the night? Where I have to flay open all my guts and let you pick through them?"

I laughed. "Not if you don't want to, but we can. That's what friends do. Your friends are people you're supposed to be able to trust with your guts."

"Literally, that's why Jax is mad at you. So are you sure you can be trusted with my guts?"

"Maybe not," I answered honestly. "I'd try really hard, though, to earn that."

"God. I was trying to make a sex joke, and you have to make it about feelings. So gross." Bastian sighed again, with an extra dose of drama.

"And yet here you are," I reminded him.

"Yes. Here I am."

"Well, if you decide to want to talk about Shae..."

"I don't."

"Okay. But if you do..."

"But I don't. No more than you want to talk about Jax."

"Except you made me do it anyway."

"Well, yes. That was for my own gratification. I like to be right." Bastian grinned at me.

"What are you right about?" Brad interjected as he slid down into the water with us.

"Besides everything?" Sebastian countered.

"You guys going to have your head in the game for Monday?" Brad asked.

"That's for sure," I said.

But it was probably another lie I'd told myself.

116

JAX

NUMBER ONE, I knew I was an asshole.

I just felt so betrayed.

I knew protection was my responsibility, too. Of course I knew that. It's just... I'd always felt like Matt was my safe place. If I couldn't handle something, he could. I kind of expected he'd... take care of me.

Wow. That was an ugly epiphany.

I realized that even though he was my best friend, I'd had him up on a kind of pedestal. I expected more from him than I did from myself.

Up until now, he'd lived up to every single one of those expectations.

He'd wanted to come with me to make it right. What else could I ask?

That maybe this hadn't happened in the first place?

My eyes watered. I didn't have to do this by myself, but I'd chosen to. If this had happened with anyone else, Matt would be the one going with me to the pharmacy. Matt would be the one holding my hand.

He still could be, but I just couldn't make myself turn around and take back what I'd said. I was still mad at him.

I was still mad at myself.

The pharmacy wasn't too far away, and I had the money to buy the pill. I reminded myself that there were many women who couldn't afford it, or women it wouldn't work for. I was lucky.

But what if, for some reason, it didn't work?

What would I do?

I thought about my mother. What would she tell me to do? I half expected my phone to ring. I half expected her to just know. When it didn't, I hadn't the most unreasonable feeling of abandonment.

I'd never felt so alone.

Then I imagined how my mother had felt, finding out she was pregnant with me after she'd just turned sixteen. How big the world must've seemed, and how small. How alone. And how incredibly fierce she had to be to raise me, and not only finish high school, but go to med school. It helped that my grandfather and grandmother were both doctors as well, but still, being a young single mother and a woman of color, even with financial advantages...

Part of me wanted to go home. I wanted my mother. Not just her words, but I wanted her hands braiding my hair. I wanted to bury my face in her shoulder and cry. I wanted my grandfather's grilled cheese, like he made for me when I was a kid. I wanted to feel the safety of home and family.

And I wanted Matt, too.

I wanted the Matt before we'd had sex. I wanted my best friend.

More importantly, I wanted *me*. The me who was so sure of herself, of what she wanted, how she was going to get it. The me who believed in lists and that with enough planning, nothing was ever left to chance.

I guess this was what adulting was about. Not getting a job and paying bills, but learning that no matter what you do, something is going to swipe the foundation right out from under you.

You may even do it yourself.

Repeatedly.

And you just have to keep building.

I went inside the pharmacy and headed back toward the counter where I saw Winter standing in line.She wore the same thing she'd had on last night, and I realized, so was I.

She arched a perfectly groomed purple brow at me and said, "You too, huh?"

I shrugged.

"Oh, sorry. I forgot the rules of Fuck Club. Rule One, don't talk about it." She snorted.

"Yeah. I guess it doesn't hurt if we're both game, and I don't see anyone else we know."

She smiled and I noticed she was actually really pretty. I mean, her aesthetic was pretty in a vampire movie kind of way. I'd thought that the first time I'd seen her, but her smile... God, I was turning into one of those people who thought everyone should smile more.

"Oh, you're not going to tell me to smile, are you?"

"No, I promise. I mean, I hope you have reasons to smile, but..." Then I couldn't help myself. "Your smile *is* really pretty, though. Your whole face changes."

"You mean as opposed to my evil, satanic, everyday look?"

"No. I think you have a very serious face, no matter how you paint it. Your smile, when you mean it, is gorgeous."

"Okay. We accept this answer as canon. We can be friends."

"Good. I mean, if we're both a member of the same club, we *should* be friends."

It was her turn in line. After she finished her transaction, she asked, "Do you want to get coffee? But not at that Black Dog place where all the preppies go. Maybe down to Donut Bar?"

"Donut bar? That sounds like the place for me."

"You've never been? Oh my god. It's amazing. And we can get cocktails. I don't know about you, but I need one."

"In the morning? Fuck it. I've had unprotected sex, might as well add day drinking to my list of infractions, right?" I said, as I paid for my pill.

"That's the spirit."

I noticed then that she had a slight accent. It was very faint. I wanted to ask her where she was from, but I didn't. She'd tell me if she wanted to. People asked me where I was from all the time, which I hated. Like, because my skin was so dark, I was something exotic. It was gross to be treated that way.

We wandered to the Donut Bar and chose a booth in the corner where we ordered a bottomless pitcher of mimosas, an assortment of donuts, savory crepes and cappuccinos.

I half expected to be carded, but the server seemed to know Winter. Her family must be important, because it was the manager who took our order. He came out from the back office after the server had seated us.

"Now that Alex knows you are my friend, you will be served anytime you come here." She winked at me.

"Does your dad own this place or something?"

"Or something." She shrugged. "So, these game nights. Do you play them every weekend? I know that in Ridgemont Hall, there was a key party?"

I nodded. "I thought about going to the key party, but... I was rather inexperienced until recently."

"I understand. I had a controlling father. I had to seduce my body-guard to get anywhere. Of course, he's been replaced since then." She shrugged again.

"It wasn't a controlling parent. It was my choice."

"Oh, good." She smiled again and shoved a donut at me. "Eat."

We opened our packages and each downed the pill we'd purchased.

"Hope this fucking thing works," Winter said. "Stupid condom broke."

"We just... yeah." I shook my head. "It was me who was stupid. Not the condom."

"Don't be so hard on yourself. We're supposed to make mistakes. That's what college is for, right?"

"I thought it was to get an education and find a career."

"Well, if you do, that's great. But really, I think it's about finding yourself. Except here's my problem. I've already found myself. I want to be an artist."

"Why is that a problem?"

"Because my father is making me do a year here before I can drop out and live the bohemian life. He thinks I should major in business, so I can help him run his empire." She snorted. "No thanks. I mean, it's great he wasn't like...oh, if you'd been a boy or any other dumb shit, but... it's not what I want."

"So what do you have to do this year? Does he have a checklist? I'm big into lists."

"I can see that." She nodded. "He actually does. Maybe you should meet my father, and you guys can talk lists, bottom lines, and trade deals. He wants me to take a few classes outside of art. I chose literature. And he wants me to have a whitebread boyfriend. No bodyguard types." She rolled her eyes. "At least he's not trying to sell me off to secure family alliances. That would suck. So, I agreed."

"A whitebread boyfriend? Like..."

"You know. Wonderbread life." She shrugged. "Someone who grew up with a yard, and a dog, and both parents at home..."

"Oh, for a second, I thought you meant white. Like...not me."

She laughed. "God, no. He doesn't care about that. Just that they have had a certain family experience. Most of them end up being guys who are into sports, and that's not me. I could actually not give less of a fuck about a bunch of grown men wrestling each other for a ball. I have nothing in common with these guys, which begs the question, why I would want to date one?"

"Have you told your father that?"

"Yes, but he doesn't really listen. I know he loves me, he just has ideas about the way things should be done."

"Well, things seemed to go well between you and Brad."

She snorted again and stuffed the rest of a donut in her mouth. "I guess. I mean, it was okay. But, like I said, we have zero in common."

"You know what you could do. You and Brad have chemistry, right? Why not have him be your pretend boyfriend? Then you can check things off your father's list. I'm sure Brad would be game."

"That's actually not the worst idea." She tapped her fingertip on her lip. "He did put his number in my phone." Her eyes narrowed. "I think my father thought I'd have to ditch the goth princess look to accomplish everything on his list. Little does he know..."

"Preppie boys love goth girls. It's like a trope, or something."

"Isn't it just?."

I ate three more donuts and drank two mimosas. With a full

stomach and a light buzz, I finally exhaled the breath it felt like I'd been holding since Matt kissed me.

"You don't know how much I needed this today," I said.

"You know, me, too. I hadn't planned on making any friends while I was here, but that's boring. Friends refill the artistic well."

"Do you draw or paint or...?"

"A little of everything. I'm very much into painting right now." Winter suddenly looked very shy. "I could show you a bit of my portfolio, if you were interested."

"Definitely."

She tapped on her phone then handed it to me.

Her work was amazing. Her sketches were so realistic, and it seemed she was able to capture the beauty of anything she put her eyes on. There was a painting of a man looking off across the quad. There wasn't anything special about him, but I found my mind making up stories to fit the painting. Adventures, trials, and victories.

"You are so talented. Why ever would anyone who loves you want you to do anything besides art?"

"I don't know." She took the phone back and tucked it into her bag. "I guess he wants me to be able to take care of myself, in case something happens to him and my trust fund. Always be prepared, he says."

"Well, if Brad doesn't work out, my best friend will play your boyfriend," I volunteered.

"Matt Graham?"

"Yeah."

"Isn't he the one you went home with?"

"I... well. Yeah. But that doesn't mean he can't be your pretend boyfriend."

"Doesn't it?"

"Let's not talk about that. I'd rather drink more mimosas."

"If we have too many more mimosas, that's going to be all you want to talk about. I'd rather get it out of the way now."

I couldn't help but smile. "Okay. Well, basically, he's mostly perfect."

"Except for last night?"

"Last night was amazing. Except for that part where we both forgot about the condom." My face heated. I was ashamed of the way I'd acted, and that I'd had him on a pedestal. He was allowed to be human, but that wasn't the only problem.

"It happens, right? That's why we have that magic pill."

"I think he's my forever, but I don't want that yet."

"Why the hell not?"

"Because I need to be wild. I never got to do that. I've always done what I'm supposed to do. I've always been a good girl, and I want to have some experiences. I'm tired of watching from the sidelines."

"That makes sense, but I think if you're with someone, you should feel like you're winning the game, not sitting on the sidelines."

"You're right about that. I guess I was looking forward to the unknown. If we decide to be together, it's like our whole lives will be mapped out already."

"Who says? It'll be going into the unknown with your best friend. What a goddamn adventure."

Maybe she was right. I still had to apologize, but I knew he'd forgive me.

And I knew he loved me.

Winter's phone started buzzing. A look of annoyance crossed her face, and she dug it out of her bag. "It's Brad. Already."

"Are you going to answer it?"

"Hell no. What kind of savage calls when he could easily text?" She turned the phone off and tossed it back into the dark depths. "Also, the morning after? Let it breathe, son."

"Wow, you rebel." I took a drink of my coffee.

"Smartass."

"Better a smartass than a dumbass."

"You got that right." Winter looked thoughtful for a moment. "You know, you may be right about Brad. Fake boyfriend thing. I mean, we could still sleep together. It *was* fun."

"Hey, why not?"

"Of course, my father is going to go through his family tree and dig up every skeleton they didn't know they had."

"You could probably pick any guy here. His family can probably trace their ancestry back to the Mayflower, and what prominent family doesn't have skeletons? Something else to consider, though. If you did actually get serious with someone, their family is going to be running checks on you, too."

"Hmm. Didn't think about that. It could cause...complications."

"I could see that." I nodded.

"Really? Do you know who my dad is?"

"I've heard rumors," I acknowledged. "But that's your business."

She exhaled heavily and leaned back against the seat. "Really, you don't care?"

"No. I like you. As wonderful as my family is, I do know that those relationships are complicated, yet we're not our parents, and we don't have to be."

"Oh good. Because I like you, too." She smiled. "And I get it. I mean, if I had a child, I wouldn't want them running around with... Well, the people my dad hangs with. They're dangerous." Her smile faded. "You know, I considered coming here under a different name. You wouldn't believe how offended my father was. He said I was shitting on my ancestry. Actually, a direct translation from Croatian was, 'You shit on your grandfather's face.'"

"That's very colorful."

"I don't understand how he expects me to have this American dream sort of experience while he's...doing what he does."

I suddenly realized that all of us were going through the same thing. Finding ourselves. My mother told me that's what college was for as much as it was about finding a career. I knew it logically, but the point had never been driven home as hard and fast as it had been in this moment.

"You're finding your way. Like we all are. I wish I could see my own path as clearly as I see yours."

"Oh, are you a psychic?" She held her palm. "Tell me, where do you see my path? Is it in my life line?" Sarcasm dripped from her words, but the smile on her face was genuine.

"You have to learn to walk a tightrope until you find that place that's the melding of your past, your history, and your future."

"Okay, Madame Zen." She snorted. "But I guess you're right. It sounds simple." Winter looked up at me, and I could see the things she'd left unspoken.

"Yeah, it sounds simple, because it is. It's just not *easy*."

"Are you done making me feel like a fuckwit who thought she had everything figured out, but really knows nothing?"

I held up my hands in mock surrender. "Hey, it's easy when it's someone else. When it comes to my own life, I'm a mess." I realized I sounded like Shae. Which was terrifying, because I thought she had all of her shit together.

"I think we're all like that, because I can fix your problem for you, too."

"Oh really?" I held my palm out to her. "Can you read my future?"

She grinned. "I can. My grandmother was Rom."

Winter snatched my hand up and studied it intently. Then she said, with the biggest smile, "Yeah, big ol' fucking mess."

"I knew that, jackass."

She laughed. "Your future holds a joyful life filled with more sunshine than rain." Winter traced her finger over my palm. "A big family. You're going to have six kids—"

"It does not! Where do you see that?"

"Hey, I just relay the message." Winter cackled. "Okay, fine. I don't actually have any clue about children. But from what my *baka* taught me, your love line is beautifully long, as is your life line. I see much happiness, much love, and a beautiful partnership that will sustain you your whole life."

Matt.

"Thanks?" I didn't know what else to say, so I ate the rest of my crepe.

"It could be worse." She shrugged.

"Aren't you supposed to say good things? Unless it's a horror movie, and you're like, oh your life line is cut—and someone lops her head off?"

"If we're doing it for money, yes. We can say 'bad' things, but only if they lead to a good outcome. People don't want to pay to be told their life is a pile of goat shit stuck in a pig's hoof."

My phone buzzed, and I knew before I checked it that it was Matt.

Matt: *I know you're not ready to talk, but when you are, I'll be here.*

Seeing his words on the screen warmed me. I'd only been away from him for a few hours and already I missed him. Already, I needed his words, his presence, everything about him more than I wanted or needed my next breath.

I couldn't have that. It was too much. Too intense. Too soon. And, not a little bit unhealthy.

Couples were supposed to be able to be apart. They were supposed to be whole people all on their own who fit together because they complemented each other's lives. They didn't *complete* them. There was a difference, and it was as wide as the ocean.

I wasn't whole without Matt.

I needed to be.

I texted back: *I'm sorry. I was shitty. I'll apologize in person, because you deserve that. I'm not ready to talk yet. I'm not punishing you. I just need more time.*

Matt: *I was going to say that not seeing you is punishment, but that's manipulative and shitty, so I'll just say I miss you.*

Matt: *I will continue to miss you.*

Matt: *I love you.*

Matt: *And I'll be here.*

I looked at the screen and studied his words. He really was too good to be true. It was so easy and right to tell him that I loved him. It was so easy to be in love with him.

Me: *I love you, too. And I miss you so much it's dumb. Talk soon.*

Talk soon? That was the dumbest thing I'd ever texted in my life. What the fuck was that even? *Talk soon.* I snorted out loud.

"More man troubles?"

"Isn't it always? My whole life, before these last two weeks could've easily passed the Bechdel Test, but everything has become about a guy. That's all my friends and I ever talk about now—relationships."

"What's the Bechdel Test?" Winter asked.

"Oh, it's a test that asks if in a work of fiction or film or whatever if there are two women present who engage in conversation about something besides a man."

"Does it apply to relationships in general? Like, two lesbians only talking about their relationships with other women? Would a book like that fail the Bechdel Test?"

"I actually have no idea, but it's an interesting question. Although, I think that would be an awesome book. It has to have a happy ending, though."

"Maybe I should write it."

"Maybe you should."

"Well, shit. Now I'm going to have to dedicate it to you."

"I can't complain. Donuts and a book dedication?"

She shoved the last donut at me. "Donut dedication."

I was full, but I ate it anyway.

It kept me from texting Matt back and making what I knew would be a huge mistake.

MATT

WHILE I WAS RELIEVED she'd forgiven me, I missed her. I couldn't think about anything but her.

I bombed Monday's game.

We all did, but I couldn't help but feel like my screw ups had been because my head hadn't been in the game. It was all about Jax. I hadn't seen her in the stands, and nothing had ever been as discouraging.

Not that I was blaming her. My failure was my own.

Everything had gone to shit. For all of us.

Unfortunately for us, we didn't have the kind of coach who said we needed to get up and try again. No, he had to break us down farther before he'd try to rebuild us.

Coach Harper basically ground us into sawdust.

We ran until we puked. We lifted weights after that. Then, we had to come back after hydrating, and run until we puked some more. After that, we ran drills. Day two, it was all drills. Day three was more running until we puked. He said we had to pay for our failure in puke.

The next game, we'd probably all just yak before it started. *There. Prepaid, bitch.*

We all felt like refried shit.

There were more kissing games tonight, but I didn't think any of us were going. We were just going to drink electrolytes and wait to die.

My phone buzzed with a text. I was tempted to ignore it. Except it might be Jax, so I picked it up.

Bastian: *Spin the Bottle. My house. Seven.*

Me: *How are you not dead?*

Bastian: *I dunno. Come play.*

Me: *I don't think so.*

Bastian: *No one told you to think. I told you to come over. Get your ass up, wash it, brush your teeth, drink some more water, and move it.*

Me: *Nuh, Bra.*

Bastian: *Motherfucker, don't make me come get you. I will.*

Me:...

Bastian: *Stop typing unless you're saying K.*

Fuck it. Fine.

Me: *K.*

Bastian: *Good.*

I dropped the phone and lay there, staring at the ceiling. I know I said I'd go, but I really just wanted to lay there some more.

I rolled out of bed, but didn't actually remember to put my feet down.

So I fell on my face.

And I laid there some more.

My phone buzzed again.

"Fuck you," I mumbled, but realized my face was actually on the floor of my dorm room.

I managed to grab the phone again.

Bastian: *I know you're not moving yet. Get. Up.*

How did he know?

Me: *I moved. To the floor.*

Bastian: *We'll start without you.*

Me: *Who is we?*

Except I had a feeling I knew exactly who was there.

Bastian: *Come see.*

Damn it. I dragged myself to the shower, and then I got dressed, cursing the whole time. I should be resting, not dragging my broken bod out to play kissing games. But that's exactly what I was doing.

I guess Coach's lesson didn't stick.

He'd worked us to death to get our mind on football, but even in this broken down, fucked up state, all I could think about was her.

Should I really be going to play a kissing game, knowing she was there, knowing she was playing, before we'd talked about everything?

Fuck it. I figured, if she was there, maybe talking about it just wasn't as important to her.

A cold splash of guilt hit me in the face. I was assuming things not directly in evidence. Maybe she still wasn't ready to talk this out.

Only, I couldn't help but wonder, what if she never was?

I'd been so sure that this couldn't break us, but what if I couldn't go back to being just friends? Especially if she didn't want to talk about what happened?

The only way to find out was to go.

It didn't take long to walk to Bastian's dorm. I'd actually considered driving because my legs were shot. Every step hurt.

Yet, nothing compared to the brick in my gut.

Bastian answered the door looking disgustingly relaxed. As if the last week hadn't happened at all. Or it was part of his regular workout routine. I wished I could be as unaffected.

"Good thing everyone likes a bit of rough now and then. Christ, you look like shit," Sebastian informed me in a faux helpful tone.

"Told you. I'm actually dying."

"It wasn't that serious."

"Maybe not for you."

"We need to get your ass back in the gym."

"Come on, you can't say that you're really not sore?"

"Sure. I'm sore, but I'm not on the verge of death like you. I thought you were just being melodramatic." He held the door wide for me to enter.

There was no one here yet, except us.

"So, starting without me, huh?"

He shrugged. "Had to say something to get you motivated."

"Is she actually coming?"

He gave me a sly grin. "I think that'll depend on us, don't you?" Then he studied me. "Although, you might not actually be up to it."

Oh, I was up to it. So. Up.

My cock was, anyway. I didn't know about the rest of my body, but I'd die trying. It would be an acceptable death.

"What, no rejoinder about how you're definitely up?" He eyed me. "Or are we doing the *I'm having complicated feelings* thing?"

"I was just thinking I might actually die, but that I was okay with it."

"Oh, good."

"Who else did you invite?"

"What makes you think I invited anyone besides you and Jax?"

"You said you were hosting a game night. You need more than three people to play Spin the Bottle or any of those games."

"Do we?" Bastian arched a brow. "This will be a different kind of a game, and a different kind of fun."

The next knock on the door reverberated through the space like the crack of thunder.

"Want to get the door while I..." he looked around "...pretend to do something so you have to talk to her?"

I laughed. "Goddamn it, Bastian."

"You're not mad at me. She won't be mad at either of us, either. You'll see."

I opened the door, and I wasn't prepared for the sight of her. Which was incredibly stupid. I knew it was her. I wanted to see her. Yet, the reality of her was so much more than what I'd expected.

She was my best friend.

She was Jax.

I was always happy to see her.

Except this was different.

The familiar shape of her, the space she occupied, her smile, her perfume, everything about her was a gut punch in the best way.

"Hi," she said, and pulled her bottom lip between her teeth.

I wanted to hug her. Kiss her. Keep her.

I wanted to tell her so many things that I ended up saying nothing of any real value. "Hey."

"Are you going to let me in?"

"I dunno. What's the password?"

"I'm afraid I've forgotten. Can't I just pay a toll?" Her smile was soft, shy, and sweet. It was almost as if the last weeks hadn't happened.

I knew a moment of sheer terror, and I glanced over her head down the hall. Escape. I could leave right now, and everything I'd feared could be put to rest. We'd fade back to what we had been—if a paler, quieter version.

"The price is always sugar, isn't it?" She rose up on her tiptoes and pressed her lips to my cheek.

The touch of her mouth on my skin reminded me why there was no going back, no fading, no pretending.

It took everything in me not to reach out and tilt her face up to mine. To kiss her so she had no doubts about my feelings, or about what I made her feel. There'd be no denying it.

Instead, I simply stepped aside and let her in.

"Where is everyone?" she asked.

When Bastian simply looked at her, I could see the knowledge dawn on her, and she scowled at me. "What is this?"

"Don't be mad at him. He had no idea."

"I said when I was ready to talk, I would. This isn't cute and—"

"No one said anything about talking, Jax. I mean, I'd love it if you two decided to handle your shit. Right now would be great, but since that doesn't look like it's going to happen, how about we just play the game? That's why you came, right?"

"Maybe I came to play the game because there would be more than just you two?" Jax pursed her lips.

Bastian was unaffected. He shrugged. "Your choice. There's the door. You don't have to stay."

She crossed her arms over her breasts, and I could see the battle going on inside her head. I knew she was thinking about playing because she wanted to see where this would lead us.

She was also still unsure after what had happened.

Yet, her pride told her to leave. To turn around and go back to her dorm and never talk to either of us again.

Her eyes slid to my face, and I knew then, too, that she was looking to me for reassurance, but then was angry at herself for doing it.

I knew her so well.

"Whatever you want, Jax."

"Isn't that what you always say, Matt? It's always about her. You basically live and breathe for that woman. What about you? Say what you want," Bastian demanded.

"I want her to be happy." It was the easiest thing in the world to say, because I meant it.

"That's not for you, Matt." Bastian leaned close to me, his breath warm on my ear, the heat of his body burning into me as he got ever closer. "What do you want? Right now. If there were no consequences?"

"There are always consequences." My voice was harsh and ragged.

"Maybe they're consequences worth living with? Don't you think, Jax?"

Jax's eyes had gone wide, her lips were parted, and she looked so torn. Afraid, confused, but aroused, too. She didn't know what to do, and I couldn't help her here. I did want her to be happy.

But I also *wanted*.

I wanted so much of everything.

I wanted her. I wanted Bastian. I wanted to see where this would go.

"I don't know," she said, still watching me.

Bastian's mouth was on my neck, and I turned into him, kissing him hard. Jax made a sound that was almost a squeak, but I couldn't quite tell over the pounding thud of my heartbeat echoing in my ears.

"Are you staying or going, Jax?" Bastian said after he broke our kiss.

"Do you want me to stay? Both of you?" she said quietly.

We still hadn't talked about anything, but that was all secondary while we burned in this fire.

"Well, I invited you both, so you know I want you here. Matt?"

Of course I wanted her to stay, but for some reason, the words got stuck in my mouth.

"Maybe I should go? This is going to screw things up more."

"If you're already screwed, you might as well enjoy the ride down," Bastian said. "He obviously wants you to stay."

"I need to hear it from him. Say the words, Matt. Tell me what you want." She stepped closer to us. "Bastian made me see just now that all of this has all been about me. About what I want. None of us ever really asked you."

"And don't say you want to make us happy. Either one of us. Say what you want for yourself. Tell me what turns you on," Bastian said.

"We'd be here all night," I finally managed, my tongue thick and heavy in my mouth.

"I've got nowhere else to be," Bastian said. "And I'm tired of you two fuckers doing this dance. We're at the ball now, and it's midnight."

"I want to watch you with her. Like at the lake."

"Good start. What else?"

Bastian's hands were moving all over my body, touching me everywhere, except where I wanted him to touch me most.

"I want you to fuck me while I fuck her."

"Oh, now we're getting somewhere," Bastian said.

Jax swallowed hard, but took another step closer to us. "What else? Would you like it if we both sucked your cock? Do you want me between you, or should I touch myself while I watch you together?"

My eyes had closed because I felt like I was watching something, participating in something that wasn't supposed to be happening to me. It was too intimate.

"Open your eyes, Matt. Look at me," she said.

I struggled to do it, so hard for both of them. For this fantasy come to life. I forgot about all my body aches, except for the one in my dick.

She dropped to her knees and Bastian pushed my shorts down, kneeling next to her.

When she took me in her mouth, my hips jerked with the sensation. Bastian met my eyes as he put his mouth on me, too. He was kissing the corner of Jax's mouth, and then both of their tongues were working my cock.

It was too much, having every fantasy I'd ever dared to imagine come to life in front of me.

I wanted them both naked.

And whatever consequences this brought, we'd all have to live with them. We'd gone too far now to turn back.

JAX

I couldn't believe we were doing this.

It was his fantasy, and mine. Ours. We were getting everything we'd wanted. Yet, I couldn't help but wonder about the emotional cost afterward.

It was a faded thing in the back of my mind, and I wasn't unaware of it, but it was secondary in the moment.

If I was honest, the only reason I'd come to the game was because I wanted to see him without the fallout. I wanted to look at him, to touch him without having to admit to any of the difficult realities.

And I'd brought condoms.

I knew we'd be drawn together, but I never thought this was something we could try together. It was one thing to talk about fantasies, it was another to live them out.

When Bastian asked what Matt wanted, at first, I'd thought... Wait, this is about *me*. I'm still angry. We need to...

But, then I thought about it. Matt always did whatever I wanted. Always.

I had never asked him what *he* wanted. Not really. I'd always assumed he'd tell me. When we were at odds, he'd waited for me to decide I wasn't angry anymore. He always put me first.

Even when he'd taken me to bed. Sure, he'd said he wanted to do it in his dorm room, in his bed, but even then, he'd made sure I got what I'd said I needed first.

Looking up at his face while Bastian and I pleasured him drove it home.

I loved him. I loved him so much it was a nearly unbearable ache in my chest. Which was really saying something, considering it drowned out the throbbing between my legs.

For better or worse, I was in love.

I knew it was possible, I knew it was even likely, but the force that knowledge hit me with was like a wrecking ball. There was no putting it off, no waiting five years. There was only now.

The tide shifted, and it wasn't about Matt anymore, like I wanted it to be. It was about me.

Both of them, with their mouths and hands all over me.

For a moment, I was afraid. There were two cocks, but only one recently devirginized space I had any interest in anything being inside.

I was pretty sure they wouldn't fit at the same time.

I mean, maybe they would. I'd seen it in porn, but I wasn't experienced.

"Let us take care of you," Bastian whispered.

"You're safe. I swear," Matt said.

I knew this was Matt asking if I'd trust him again. If I really had forgiven him. "I know."

I surrendered to my wildest fantasy. I let them take me as high and as far as they wanted. There was such freedom in that surrender. I was lost on a sea of ecstasy and sensation.

They'd both dipped their heads between my thighs, and I was torn between wanting to lie back and experience what they were doing to me, and watching them together. Their tongues tangled with each other while they licked me and it was the most erotic thing I'd ever seen, but I had the feeling before the night was over, something else was going to win that title.

I rode those waves of pleasure until I was incoherent. I may have called out in tongues. I may have invoked gods, demons, curses and blessings. I didn't know.

All I knew was that when I lay there, completely wrung out, Matt's voice was silky seduction in my ear. "Do you still want this?"

What he meant was *do you still want me?*

"Only if we're living out your fantasy. Is he going to fuck you while you fuck me?"

"Yes."

God, I'd thought I was done with orgasms, but they weren't done with me. I hadn't thought I could feel the flaring heat again, not so soon after being burned to ash, but it rose to a glorious flame.

Every nerve ending was on fire. I was overstimulated, but I still needed more.

I heard the tell-tale rip of two condom packages being torn open. Matt was on top of me, and then inside me.

He froze, solid and stiff, and I saw Bastian behind him, one big hand on his shoulder. Matt bore his weight, and I heard Sebastian's ragged whisper. "Relax. Breathe. I'll go slow."

The three of us were captured in the moment like dragonflies in amber.

Until I giggled.

"Jesus, now is not the time," Bastian chastised me.

"It really is. We both lost our virginity to you."

Matt snickered, but then closed his eyes as he exhaled sharply.

"Does that feel good? Tell me," Bastian demanded.

The symbiosis of what was happening between us had just stolen the crown of most erotic thing. The expression on Matt's face, feeling his body tense and his cock surge inside me as he hit his pinnacle right there was overwhelming.

He was graceful in his collapse as he crashed down on his back next to me.

"Goddamn it," he swore, his breathing ragged.

"You're not done yet," I told him. "But you can tap out for a round."

"Let me clean up." Bastian was on his feet and headed toward the bathroom. I heard the water running.

It was strange how, even though we'd done something so very intimate, I'd never felt father away from Matt. It was like we needed

Bastian to be close. Maybe it was because we hadn't talked, because we still had so much to unpack and sort out.

But I decided fuck that, because he was always going to be my best friend. I reached out and twined my fingers with his. He squeezed back.

"That, um, didn't go as anticipated."

"No? What would you change about it?"

"I would've lasted a lot longer." He sort of laughed. I could tell he was embarrassed.

"When it's good, it's good, right?"

"Yeah. And it was *good*."

"Thanks," I said.

"For what?" He hadn't let go of my hand.

"For sharing that with me."

"I guess it's only fair. I mean, I saw your moment."

"I'd say this was a million times different, but I'm glad we were here together."

"Me, too."

"Are you two talking now?" Bastian emerged from the bathroom, water still on his skin, but a new condom package in his hand. "Because, really, that's what I was going for."

"Was it really? Or was this, right here, what you were going for?" I asked him.

He shrugged. "Well, you know. It had a good result nonetheless."

I met Bastian's eyes. "Let's give him the rest of what he wanted."

Bastian grinned. "You got it."

Matt and I kept holding hands. It was ridiculous, but it wasn't. I was lost in Bastian, but I had Matt's hand holding me, reminding me where the earth was, even while I was flying.

I thought that would mean being chained down, but it let me fly higher.

Freer.

His gaze on Bastian and me, when it turned hot again, when he used his other hand and stroked his cock watching us, it didn't tame me. It didn't hold me back or diminish what I felt in the moment.

In fact, it turned me on.

God, it turned me on.

I'd never unsee that moment, him spilling into his hand while another orgasm rocked my body.

We spent the night together, the three of us.

In the morning, Bastian actually kicked us out.

"Well, kids. It's been real. It's been fun, but... Actually, it *has* been real fun. But I need to sleep, and for you two to get the hell out." His tone was light and teasing, but he meant it.

"What?" I asked. I was actually a bit incredulous.

"Yes, darling. Out. I love you, which is why you have to go. No feelsies, remember? Now, we're all the best of friends, and you two can go hash thing out. Next weekend, we're playing at my place for real. Seven in Heaven. Or maybe Never Have I Ever."

"I didn't think Never Have I Ever was a kissing game?" Matt asked.

"It is the way I play it." Bastian grinned. "Now, seriously. You've got to go." He shooed us. "Go out to coffee. Talk about all the babies you're going to have in a hundred years. I don't know. Just go."

I hugged him tightly and kissed his cheek.

So did Matt.

"We love you, too."

"See? This is why we can only be friends, now." Bastian waved his hand. "And this is forever, I hope you know. You made me have a feeling, so you're dealing with it as long as I have it."

"Good," I said and hugged him again.

Except when we left, we were both silent and awkward.

He finally said, "So do you want to go first?"

"Okay." I took a deep breath. "First off, you look like shit."

"Thanks?"

"I'm sorry I wasn't at the game." I pressed my lips together. "I just...couldn't."

"We sucked. We sucked a lot. All of us. It was the worst game I've ever played."

"Is that why Bastian hosted an impromptu retreat to...what was it you called it, Fuck Island?"

"Uh, no. Fuck Island was your terminology. *All* yours."

"Well, do you think it was?"

"No. I think he... well, maybe. I guess we could ask him the next time we see him."

It wasn't too long before we were at my dorm pod, and we hadn't really started talking. This was all Walk of Shame small talk. Not that I was actually ashamed of anything I'd done, but you know, wandering back to your dorm in the same clothes you'd left in the night before... Yeah.

"We're here." I felt incredibly stupid for stating the obvious.

"Yeah."

We stood there for a long moment. "This is dumb," I said. But still, nothing else came to my lips.

He gave me an easy out. "Maybe it's not the right time to talk."

"But then when will be?"

"If you had something you wanted to say, you'd say it, wouldn't you? I think that speaks for itself, doesn't it?"

Was he right?

It had been pretty easy last night to tell him to fuck me harder. Why then, when it came to telling him what I wanted, would it be hard to say the words?

Unless I didn't actually know what I wanted, which was unfair to both of us.

"I don't know. What about you? Aren't there things you want to say that you aren't saying?"

"You asked me to give you space. That's what I'm trying to do."

"Last night was the farthest thing from space as you can get, Matt."

"Hey, I didn't set that up."

"So, you're not going to take any ownership of what happened?" I asked, my chest tightening and my stomach turning on itself.

"I thought that was the point of the game. We don't have to take ownership of what happens."

"Is that really how you want to do this?" I whispered.

"What do you want me to say, Jax? I told you that I love you. I told you that I miss you. You said you wanted space and you'd talk when you were ready. You're not talking. What am I supposed to do with that?"

"Okay, I'm ready to talk."

"Okay."

We still stood there staring at each other.

We both laughed, but it wasn't funny. It was heartbreaking. "It's never been hard to talk to you before and I don't know what to say."

"Like I said, maybe it's not the right time to talk."

Except, I had this horrible feeling if I took that at face value, that it would never be the right time to talk. We wouldn't drift back to old habits. We'd splinter apart, and it'd be like losing a piece of myself.

I started to doubt he felt the same way about me. About our friendship. If maybe he'd just decided this wasn't what he wanted at all. Maybe this was the easy way out. The escape hatch.

Who was I to deny him?

Besides the woman who was in love with him.

It hadn't occurred to me until this moment that maybe having these other kinds of feelings for me would make him feel trapped, too. I'd just sort of assumed, after he'd shown interest, that if I wanted him, he was mine.

"I feel like if we don't talk, we're done," I blurted.

"Maybe we are. Maybe this was just a fluke. But we'll always be friends."

His words sounded hollow to me.

"Maybe I don't want to be friends. Maybe I want to be yours, and I want you to be mine."

"I don't think that's what you really want. I think you're just afraid of losing us."

Suddenly, I understood. "Oh. You don't want that."

"Neither of us knows what we want, not really, Jax. I mean, what happened, could that have happened if we were together? I know you still have a lot of things to try and experience. Maybe I do, too."

"I don't understand why we can't do it together. Like last night."

"What if I were to call one of the girls in my phone for another threesome tonight. How would that feel? Is that okay?"

A cold wash of jealousy coursed through me.

"Or what if I were to call someone for date? Just me and that other person. Male or female. Because I know you don't want to give up your autonomy. I'm supposed to be okay with that for you, but I can already see the way your eyes are narrowing that it wouldn't be okay for me."

"Okay. Maybe you're right. Maybe I do need to think about this more. But I don't want to go back to being just friends. I don't think we can."

"But I don't think we can move forward, either, so where does that leave us?"

"I don't know." My nose tingled like someone had punched me in the face. "I love you."

"I love you, too."

Except he wasn't touching me. He didn't hug me. He didn't hold my hand.

"I have one more thing to say to you." I lifted my chin. "I wasn't going to, but I don't know if I'm going to get the chance again to tell you. I don't just love you, Matt. I'm in love with you."

He closed his eyes and took a deep breath. "Too bad you couldn't have realized that sooner."

"Why? So you could walk away sooner?"

"For both of our sakes," he said.

Then, I got angry. "Why for both of our sakes? So what if we don't have everything figured out? We'd find our boundaries. Our hard limits. And maybe that would be by blowing past them, and maybe that would hurt for a while, but we'd make it through. If we wanted to."

"Maybe I don't want that kind of relationship. Maybe I want something safe. Maybe what I want is what you'd settle for."

His words sliced me. I thought I knew him inside and out. Only, maybe I didn't.

"Is that what you want?"

"That's what I'm trying to tell you, Jax. I don't know."

"Can't we figure it out together?" I tried one last time.

"No. Because one of us would end up settling for half of what we wanted just so we wouldn't lose the other."

"You told me I could never lose you."

"Maybe I was wrong."

"Why are you mad at me? I don't understand."

A freshman I didn't know stopped and looked at us, but when I fixed her with a death glare, she scurried down the corridor.

"Because I don't like being wrong. Because I don't want to be what you settle for. And I don't want to settle either."

"How is that my fault?"

"It's not your fault, but you changed."

"We both did. That's what we're supposed to do."

"Maybe we didn't change in a way that our pieces still fit together."

I thought about my own conclusions earlier. About how we both had to be whole on our own. That we fit together best as whole pieces instead of jagged shards.

"Oh, we fit together just fine, fucker. You're so lucky I'm not giving up on you. I'm tempted, but you'll see."

Only, I wasn't so sure.

"Jax, this isn't like every other thing where you just decide what you want and I give it to you."

"Why not? You started a trend, and now I expect you to follow through."

"I don't know if I can."

I tried to keep my costume of bravado in place, but it fell away so easily. "Don't you love me?"

"Of course I do."

"Then that's all that matters, isn't it?"

"If only it were that easy."

And the bastard left me standing there in front of my dorm room, alone.

MATT

Everything had gone to shit.

If I'd thought things sucked before, they were now in Sucktown, Capital of Sucksitania.

I didn't want her to choose me, to choose "us," just because she was afraid of losing me. I knew I deserved better than that, and so did she.

But damn it, the look on her face.

She looked like I kicked her in the stomach, and even though I felt that same way, I didn't want to hurt her. She'd said she was in love with me, and it hurt all the more because I wanted it.

I walked back to my dorm slowly.

I realized, while I was walking, the world has lost its color. I knew logically the sky was blue and the grass was green, but everything without her was gray.

I couldn't get the look on her face out of my head.

I'd fucked up. I'd just assumed I knew her better than she knew herself. I'd been doing that all along.

Part of me wanted to run back to her, to beg her forgiveness, to hear her tell me she loved me again.

But that didn't address the problems we would still have.

I wouldn't lie to myself and pretend like the threesome wasn't the hottest thing that had ever happened to me, but I didn't know if I wanted to have an open relationship like she'd suggested.

It wasn't that I didn't trust her. Of course, I trusted her. It was that maybe I didn't trust myself to be able to get past my ego, and how I'd been taught was a relationship was supposed to be. I didn't know if I wanted to.

I had this idea of my future, and it didn't include swinger's parties.

I mean, maybe when I was fourteen it did, but this wasn't only about lust and fantasy. It was about building the whole of a life. Which neither of us were ready to start doing, or so I'd thought.

Except, when I thought about my future, she was always part of it. When I'd decided that eventually I wanted to be married, to have a family, it was always Jax at one side and some other unknown woman on the other. This unknown woman was always some fey idea. A placeholder.

But that was gone. It was only Jax.

Which was too bad for me, because I couldn't stuff her in the premade box of what I'd decided I wanted. She was who she was.

And I was who I was.

My phone buzzed, and I pulled it out of my pocket.

Jax: *I'm going to give you some space, but there's more I need to say to you.*

Me: *K.*

Jax: *K? Bitch, K?*

Jax: *I don't even get your stupid, irritating okay? I deserve the other three letters.*

I found myself smiling even though my heart was still breaking.

I hit the voice option. "Okay."

Jax: ...

Jax: *Well, that's something.*

Me: *So, I realized I made a mistake. Trying to choose for you. That was wrong, but I do need to think. I need to choose for me.*

Jax: *You made me cry. You haven't done that since middle school.*

Jax: *I don't like it. It's unapproved.*

Me: *I'm sorry.*

Jax: *Apologies don't count unless they're in person.*

Me: *Don't you still owe me one? You said you'd give it to me in person.*

Jax: *You don't think the five rounds of sex we just had was an apology?*

Me: *Nope. That's the easy answer.*

Jax: *Fine. Come back here.*

That was the thing I couldn't do, wasn't it? It'd be so easy to turn around and go back to Jax. Back to the person who brought light to my world. Back to the woman I loved.

Me: *I shouldn't. I need to think.*

Jax: *You can't think when you're with me? I remember when I was your safe place. You always said I made your brain quiet.*

Me: *You do. And when I'm with you, I can't hear my head. Just my dick and my heart.*

Jax: *That's both the sweetest and most fucked up thing you've ever said to me.*

Matt: *Want another?*

Jax: *Fuck it. Why not? I'm already crying.*

I realized I was, too.

Me: *Me too.*

Jax: *Then what the hell are you doing? Come back. Blanket fort.*

I didn't respond. If I gave myself the chance to do anything except turn around, I wouldn't do it. Except going back to her was an act of self-preservation.

It wasn't too long before I knocked on the door.

"Not today."

"It's me."

She flung open the door. "I didn't think you were coming. You didn't answer."

"When your best friend says 'blanket fort,' you're not allowed to say no."

She launched herself at me in a fierce, tight hug. I caught her and didn't want to let go. We just held each other there.

It wasn't about anything in that moment except not letting go.

We still had to talk, but we could do that after the blanket fort. I exhaled, and so did she. It was like neither of us could breathe without the other.

"I'll get the stuff for the fort," she mumbled into my neck.

I didn't want to let go, not even to get the stuff for the fort. How had I ever thought I had a choice when it came to being with her? I could choose no, sure. But why would I ever choose a life without her?

She untangled herself from me and went to the closet where she pulled out an ancient card table we'd been using since we were kids. It wasn't very big. She still fit underneath it fine, but my feet had been sticking out since freshman year of high school.

I helped her throw a blanket over the top, and we crammed pillows underneath before we crawled inside.

"Do you remember how we used to pretend this was a stagecoach or a vardo?" she asked me.

"Yeah. I'd be the outlaw trying to rob the couch, and you always saved the day," I said.

"There was that one time I let you rob the coach," she said, laughing.

"Yeah, but only if I took you to Mexico, where you could be an outlaw, too." I smiled, remembering. "Do you remember the one where you were Cinderella?"

"You were Prince Charming."

"With my pelican head."

"That was the last time we played those games in the blanket fort."

"Yeah, I remember you said we were too old for pretend."

She looked down and her hands folded in her lap. "You're never too old for pretend."

"Then why did you say we were?"

"Because that's when I wanted you to be my Prince Charming, and I knew you didn't think about me that way," she confessed.

"You're right, I didn't. You were Jax." I shrugged. "I wasn't even thinking about girls then."

"I beg to differ. Remember when I was getting a pair of your shorts and found that skin mag?"

I coughed. "Listen, those weren't girls."

"Oh really? I hope some objectifying misogynist nonsense is not about to come out of that mouth."

I laughed. "No, no. Not at all. I don't know if I can explain it. They were women. Obviously." I coughed again. "They were images of some-day. The girls in school, they were right now. None of them were remotely interested in me. I knew what I looked like. I'd watched all the same movies you did, and it did not look good for Pelican Head."

"I guess that makes sense."

This place was safe, our blanket fort. Here we were, after every-thing that had happened, sitting the way our grade school teachers had called "criss-cross-applesauce" and that's how I knew that maybe everything would be okay.

"I can't believe I never realized you liked me like that, then."

"I am so glad." She laughed. "I'd never been more grateful for some-thing in all of my life." Jax was quiet for a moment. "When we first started talking about things, you said that you'd fantasized about me."

"Oh god, you're demanding details, aren't you?" I'd tell her, if she really wanted to know.

"Not yet." She grinned. "I kind of like where we are right now. It's just us again. The us that we know. But I do want to know when the first time was." She reached out and took my hand.

"The very first?"

"Oh, is this juicy? Let's have it."

"You just want me to stroke your ego."

"Yes, I do. Gimme." The open smile on her face was the one that always made me want to give her anything she wanted, just so it would stay.

"Fine. It was the pool party at the country club for your birthday."

"What?"

"That white bikini. Jesus Christ, that thing should've been regis-tered as a weapon." I closed my eyes thinking of it.

"No. What? Really?" She laughed. "Was that why you kept chasing me so you could throw me in the pool?"

"No. I really just wanted to throw you in the pool."

"Ass. Well, spill."

"We were in the water. Your suit came untied."

"You swam up behind me and fixed it. You said no one saw anything."

"No one did. The goods were covered." I reassured her.

"So, why did that give you a case of the bone to think about?"

"Your back was bare. I don't know. The way your skin felt while I tied the string. I can't explain it."

"I remember you got out of the pool pretty fast after that."

"Yeah. Because my dick was going to explode. I felt so guilty about that for a long time."

"Confession is good for the soul. Feel better?" She grinned.

"No. Not at all."

"So after you beat your body into submission, then what?"

"Maybe we don't need to tell each other everything."

"Oh, no. We totally do. You're not getting out of telling me this." She crossed her arms. "I'm waiting."

"Fine. I started having dreams about you last summer."

"Why didn't you tell me? That's not an active choice on your part. You don't get to choose what your brain does in your dreams."

"No, but I can choose what it does when I'm awake. When I was awake, I did choose to think about you."

"Good."

"Good? I was in hell. I felt like such a shit."

"I'll tell you something. You know that time in the pool? I'd never wanted anyone to touch me so badly before or since. Just your fingertips brushing against my back like that..."

"I can't imagine the fuckall of a mess we would've made of things then," I said.

"Not unlike where we are now?" she said quietly.

"Let's not talk about now yet. I missed our blanket fort. I missed you."

"Okay. Me, too. Then what should we talk about?"

"Well, now it's weird. It's like asking where you want to eat dinner."

"Pizza, obviously. There. Next."

"Okay. Come here." I shifted and pulled her against me, and she rested her head on my chest. "Your hair still smells like coconut."

"And you smell like fuck boy. What is that body wash? Badass Badger?"

"Eh, close enough."

"I'm ashamed by how much I like it."

"That's why I use it."

We lay there quietly for what felt like a years, but I didn't have any desire to move. To break the moment. Because if we did, we'd have to move forward, and I still didn't know which path I should take.

Or, if I was being completely honest, whether I could even see a path.

It just felt good and right to hold her.

"Can we stay here?"

"I think so. At least until Monday."

She laughed, but burrowed closer.

I stroked my hand down her back, and her fingers played with the bottom edge of my t-shirt in a comforting and familiar rhythm.

"This is home," she said. "Whatever else happens, this is home."

I should've known then, no matter what happened, that this wasn't the brain's choice anymore. Our hearts had decided, and the rest was just along for the ride.

Instead, I said, "I guess we should get around to that talking, huh?"

"I'm sorry," she said. "I never apologized in person for what happened. I was really scared and betrayed, but that wasn't actually your fault. I betrayed myself. It was my biggest fear. Not that someone would do something to me, but that I'd be so caught up that I'd do it to myself. And I did. Truthfully, it wasn't the worst thing that could've happened. So, forgive me, okay?"

"You knew you were already forgiven as soon as it happened. I understand. And I'm sorry, too. I should've thought about it, too."

"And...?" she prompted.

"And what?"

"You said you were going to apologize for earlier."

"No one said you were getting apology today."

She squeezed me tighter. "You better."

"Or?"

"I haven't devised a punishment yet, but rest assured it will be vast and mighty."

I kissed her forehead. "Okay, I'm sorry for earlier, too. For not accepting that you do actually know your own mind and are perfectly capable of making your own decisions."

We were quiet for some time longer.

"Where does that leave us, Matt? We're both sorry. Now what?"

"Now, we try not to keep making the same mistakes that made us sorry."

"Remember that time when we were visiting your cousins and they took us to the lake?"

"I remember I got in the worst trouble of my life. My father explained to me in his serious voice that I could've died. We both could've. And it would've been my fault." That wasn't something I'd ever forget.

"Oh god, it wouldn't have been your fault. We both decided to jump off that rock." She pulled back so she could look up me. "Do you remember the jump?"

"We were both terrified. So, we held hands, and we both screamed all the way down to the water. I'm surprised we didn't drown since our mouths were open."

"I'm surprised we didn't get dysentery. Your cousins were evil little shits who should've told us that it was...unclean. That wasn't the point, though. The point was that we jumped together. We fell together. Here and now... did I fall alone?"

I knew this was it. The do or die moment. There wouldn't be any more picking it to death. All I had to do was say she did. That she'd tripped and fell all by herself.

But then there'd be no more blanket forts either. No more Jax.

No more home.

"It's backwards here, though. We had to fall, and now we have to jump."

"We do, and I want you to jump with me, Matt. Even if we scream all the way down."

"Even if we drown?" I asked her.

"Even if we get dysentery and then we drown. There is no one's hand I'd rather be holding. There is no one I'd rather jump with. We'll figure out the details on the way down. Just like we did then."

"Fine. But we're really getting married when we're thirty on a beach in Grand Cayman. You're going to wear a white bikini."

"If I knew that's all it took to get you, I would've never worn anything else." She tilted her face to me.

When I kissed her, it was more than a kiss.

It was a jump off a cliff where I couldn't see the bottom. But it didn't matter, because Jax was holding my hand, and I was holding hers.

JAX

WE'D MADE it harder than it needed to be, but I guess that's what everyone does when they're young. I remembered my mother's advice about how no one could define our relationship but us.

Having decided that what happened with Bastian had happened organically, we were open to other experiences together, if they happened the same way. We weren't going to put any limits on each other except honesty and love.

We didn't have to lock everything down right now. Not so long as we agreed to keep communicating and keep loving each other.

We were both afraid at first, but it's been a month and nothing is really different, except that we have more secret glances and a lot of amazing sex.

I kind of think that this is where happily ever starts, but I'm not sure. Whatever it is, I'm on the bus until after the wheels fall off.

"Hey, did you hear that Pandora and Conrad are hosting a game of Seven in Heaven tonight in the common room?" Matt called to me as he stepped out of the shower.

"Oh, do you wanna go play?" I teased him.

"Maybe." He grinned, his wet hair falling forward on his forehead and water sluicing down his face. "Or maybe we should just stay in."

I'll admit, I was tempted. Stay in, eat more pizza, and have the best sex of my life with my best friend or go to some silly party with kissing games and think again how lucky I am that everything I want is right here?

He kissed me hard. Stole my breath.

"Or maybe we should do both?"

"I like that plan," I murmured against his mouth and tugged on the towel around his waist. "Then, afterward, more pizza."

"It's always about more with you."

"And you keep giving it to me."

"Always," he said. Then he proved it and kissed me some more.

Yeah, I thought while he pushed me down on his bed, this was indeed where happily ever started.

SEVEN IN HEAVEN BLURB

The fun and games continue at Ridgemont Hall with *Seven in Heaven*. Keep with the RH gang by signing up for my newsletter here: www.sarawylde.com

Seven in Heaven
    Fast Times at Ridgemont Hall #3

Bonnie

I really thought going to a party at the illustrious Ridgemont Hall would be more refined than kid's kissing games in closets. Until my best friend's older brother is the one I'm locked in a closet with for seven minutes. Those seven minutes were both heaven and hell. I got the make-out session I've been dreaming of for the last four years, but things get complicated. (Don't they always?) I want more from Justin than seven minutes. (Don't we all?) But I don't know that he has it to give.

Justin

I only wanted to show her that she was playing with fire, but it was me who got burned. I can't keep my hands off her, and what's worse is she tells me I don't have to. She's offering me everything I never knew I wanted. Bonnie has always been like a kid sister to me, but suddenly she's a wildcat of a woman. Whenever I try to reconcile this new Bonnie with little Bon-Bon, I feel like I'm crossing a sacred line. I should be protecting her, especially from myself. If only that seven minutes in heaven wasn't worth burning in hell.

SEVEN IN HEAVEN SNEAK PEEK

Bonnie

*J*ustin St. Cyre had been the star of my every fantasy since I was fifteen.

I really wanted that to change.

It wasn't actually getting me anywhere. I was stuck in a Justin loop. Especially since his little sister was my best friend. Guess where that left me?

I wasn't invisible to him. No, he saw me. He saw me like another little fungus following him around, needing his protection from the big scary men.

In high school, I hadn't dated anyone. I thought it was because I was ugly for the longest time. Until I found out from Justin that he'd told every guy who'd ever expressed interest in me that he'd "fuckstart their head" if they so much as laid one little finger on me.

Which wouldn't have bothered me in the least, if it had been for some other reason besides the fact he saw me as a child.

I'd fixed that in these last few weeks of playing the Ridgemont Hall kissing games. Justin St. Cyre didn't even know I was here. I'd asked Rachel not to tell him.

Of course, if I was being honest, I'd picked Ridgemont to get the farthest I could from home. I had this stupid fantasy that, one day, he'd look at me and realize I was a woman. He'd throw me over his giant shoulder and carry me off into the sunset. Or something.

Rachel had gotten into Harvard, so while Hollingsworth was a good school, it wasn't Harvard. I didn't have the grades or actually anything special to recommend me. I mean, my grades were decent, but I wasn't the over-achieving crackhead on paper that Rachel was. So, it was off to Harvard for her and Hollingsworth for me.

I already missed her so much, even though we talked almost every day through some form of media or another. Usually, it was text. Sometimes it was private messages on social media platforms.

Even though we were in the same dorm—I don't know why Justin had wanted to be in Ridgemont, but whatever—I didn't see him often. Which was good. I hadn't exactly said hello.

I almost literally ran into him in the bookstore, but I'd made a quick exit. I'd been terrified to go to that game of Spin the Bottle at Shae Edgecomb's apartment, because I'd thought that Justin might be there.

He didn't seem to be into the kissing games or the parties, which was really too bad for me. No chance of the bottle landing on him and me getting my fantasy come to life.

Yeah, he was my fantasy, but I was avoiding him. Why? The whole *fuckstart your head* thing. I didn't need that shitting on my chances of making memorable mistakes while in college. Honestly, if he did that again, I'd probably change schools.

I had to establish myself first. *Then* I could make cow eyes at him, for all the actual good it would do me.

I've had some great kisses. I'd let Brooklyn Chase punch my v-card, which all in all had been nice. Nothing to really write home about.

Rachel lost hers the same weekend, except she was convinced she was in love with this guy. Who knows? Maybe she really was. I thought it was too soon, but she seemed so happy, so I'd keep that to myself. Unless she asked for my opinion, I'd just be happy for her.

"Little Bon Bon, I'm starting to think you're ignoring me." Justin's deep voice startled me, and I promptly dropped my messenger bag. It did me the singular honor of falling open, sending my laptop, phone, and makeup bag spilling out across the concrete.

He did the big brother thing, of course. "Let me help."

Justin started picking up my things. The lipstick that rolled away from the makeup bag and...oh god. That wasn't lipstick.

Oh my god.

Oh my god.

Oh my god.

It was the pocket vibe made to look like a lipstick tube at first glance. Rachel bought it for me as a gag gift for graduation. I got her a butt plug with a raccoon tail. We'd thought I'd won that round, but this one—this had come back to haunt me.

He picked it up casually.

My whole world stopped to a single, narrow point. His fingers on my vibe.

I was torn between mortification and instant, blinding lust.

My mouth hung open like a gate on a rusty hinge. It probably squeaked as I tried to form coherent words, but nothing came out.

Then he just dropped it in the bag, like it was nothing more than lipstick. Maybe he didn't know. I was praying to every deity above, below, and in between that he just had zero clue.

When we'd crammed everything back into my messenger bag, he said, "Didn't mean to scare you, Bon."

"I..." I was about to say he hadn't, but he so obviously had. "I've been really caught up in finding my way around and studying. You know how hard classes are here the first year."

"Why didn't you tell me you were coming here?" He narrowed his eyes. "Why didn't Rachel?"

"I wanted to find my way on my own. I was going to say hi eventually." I grinned up at him.

God, why did he have to be so beautiful? He was tall, with caramel hair, and amber eyes... yeah, I know. Amber eyes. Doesn't happen in nature. But his did. He was all tan and... He was actually the most beautiful human I'd ever seen alive.

No, actually he was more beautiful than any magazine model, too.

Plus, he smelled vaguely of chocolate today.

"Why do you smell like chocolate?" I blurted.

His smile bloomed. "It was a wild weekend." He winked at me.

My whole body fluttered like a drunk butterfly.

"It's about to get a lot wilder with you walking around on campus smelling like chocolate this early in the morning, I tell you what."

He laughed. "You're adorable, Bon Bon, you know that? I missed you. Come here."

Suddenly, he was hugging me, and I wasn't sure if I was in heaven or hell.

I figured fuck it. Whichever place I was, I might as well enjoy the benefits.

He smelled so good. He body felt like velvet wrapped bricks that had been left out in the sun. He was so hot and hard.

I know, it was creepy I was perving on him while he was hugging me. I hated it when guys did that to me. They'd try to hug me just to mash themselves against my substantial breasts. So gross.

Yet, here I was doing it to Justin.

He released me, and I wasn't too happy about it.

"Well, you know if you need anything at all, I'm just a text away. Okay?"

"Yeah. Thanks." I pressed my lips together, debating if I should say what was next on the tip of my tongue. "You know I appreciate that you look out for me and have taken on the big brother role..." I began.

"But you don't want me to tell anyone I'm going to fuckstart their head if they talk to you?" He laughed. "That's really why you didn't tell me you were coming to Hollingsworth. And why you didn't talk to me in the bookstore."

"Guilty."

"I do so solemnly swear not to interfere in your dating life unless requested." He held up his hand. "Scouts' Honor."

"Good. Because I've had to work really hard to catch up on all the things I missed in high school."

He just quirked a brow at me. Then he said, "Don't tell me you're in Ridgemont Hall."

"Okay. I won't tell you." I shrugged.

"Bon."

"What? You're in Ridgemont Hall, too. And, apparently, you've been up to dirty things in chocolate. I'm not judging *you*."

He put his arm around me. "Ah, you know I just want to look out for you. No judgment. You're Rachel's best friend. She'd kill me if anything bad happened to you."

"She'll kill you if you interfere with my autonomy. And then so will I."

"You're all grown up now, are you?" he teased. "You're never too grown for an older brother."

"Maybe I am. How about we be friends, instead?"

"Nah. Friends can be temporary. Family is forever." He squeezed my shoulder.

I got another waft of chocolate and my mouth watered.

"I guess I'll let you have that one. But you know what? You owe me some chocolate."

Justin laughed again. "Yeah, all right. I assume it's going to be cheesecake from that place downtown?"

"Wait... what place?"

"Hmm. I don't know if I should introduce you to those sinful delights or not," he teased.

The idea of him introducing me to any sinful delights made me bite my lip. "When are you going to pay up?"

"Friday night."

"Hmm. I can't Friday. Plans."

"Don't tell me. You're going to play Truth or Dare?" He rolled his eyes.

"Maybe." I grinned.

"Fine. How about before the game?"

"Done."

Suddenly, one of the most beautiful women I'd ever seen came up to Justin and tucked herself under his arm. "Hey, there."

"Hey, yourself. Bonnie, this is Catriona. She's the other TA in that ethics class." He turned to her. "Bonnie is kind of like my little sister."

I rolled my eyes again.

"She doesn't look so little to me." Catriona gave me a genuine smile, and I was glad this wasn't going to be some catfight over a man's attention. A lot of his girlfriends had been that way. They resented any time he gave to Rachel and they *definitely* resented any time he gave to me. They were always trying to get rid of us.

"Thanks for noticing. Legally, I'm an adult, but I've been Rachel's best friend since we were in diapers."

"Oh! Rachel is pretty great. I got to meet her the last time Justin was home. You were in Paris, then, right?" She turned to Justin. "Why do you smell like chocolate? Wait, don't tell me."

"So, you're not the one he engaged in illicit chocolate things with? Color me surprised. I thought you were his girlfriend."

Catriona laughed. "Oh my god, no. I mean, no offense. I love him dearly, but danger worms aren't my happy place."

I snorted. "Excuse me, what?"

"I'm a lesbian."

"Oh. Well then. I just assumed...sorry."

"No worries." She smiled. "Hey, she should come with us on the campout Saturday."

"I think she's busy." Justin looked at me. "But, if you want, you can come."

I couldn't tell if he actually wanted me to go, or if the *I think she's busy* meant *don't come*.

"A campout? I've never actually been camping, so it might be cool." This would give him the opportunity to tell me how much I wouldn't like it, if he didn't actually want me to go. I didn't want to inflict myself on him and his friends.

"It's definitely cool. We're going to be taking water and soil samples for Environmental Engineering. We'll be testing them for pesticides, heavy metals, and other contaminants. I'm excited. This class has made me rethink my focus from Environmental Law to Engineering. I like the hands-on approach. I feel like I'm doing more." The excitement on his face was contagious.

"Yeah, I'll come. It sounds awesome."

"Great!" Catriona said. "I have an extra tent you can use, if you don't mind a single."

"Nah, this is her first time. She can sleep with me. Bonnie can graduate to her own tent next time, if she likes it."

She can sleep with me.

Why yes, yes I could. This couldn't have turned out more perfectly if I'd planned it. Actually, if I'd tried to plan it, it would've been a shit-show on wheels.

"Where are you headed?" Catriona asked me.

"I have a free period for study."

"I'll walk you to the library," she said.

Justin smiled at me again, and I melted all the way down into a puddle in my shoes. "Already making friends. See? Hanging out with me isn't so bad. See you later, Bon Bon."

I didn't want to walk away from him. I could've sat there, basking in the wattage of his smile, all day. Something I'd frequently done as a kid.

"So, I hope you don't mind me getting really personal really fast."

I laughed. "Not at all. With some people you just know, right?"

"Yeah. You really do." She took a deep breath and then exhaled slowly. "I'm not usually such a tool."

"I am, so it's fine."

She laughed. "Rachel is your best friend, right?"

"Last time I checked."

"Is she seeing anyone?" Catriona blurted, then she blushed. "I mean, would she ever go out with a woman?"

I shipped this instantly. Catriona was beautiful, obviously smart, and there was something about her that immediately felt familiar and warm. If I believed in past lives, I'd say that we'd always known each other. The same way Rachel and I, it had seemed, had always known each other.

"We've never actually talked about it. She's dating some guy right now, who I haven't met, but I already kind of hate."

She groaned. "Why do I always have to fall for straight girls? What's wrong with me? I thought we had a moment that weekend, but I guess not, if she didn't say anything to you about it. I mean, not that I'd expect you to tell me, but if we had, and she'd told you, you might make me more inclined to think she would go out with me. Shit, I'm babbling."

"It's kind of nice, actually, to see someone who looks like you all flustered."

"Well, it doesn't matter what I look like if I don't have the equipment she's looking for. That really sucks."

"Hey, you don't know that. Maybe she didn't tell me about it because she was unsure of how she felt about it. She tells me most everything, but I know she's got her own secrets, and I know I have mine. Like any normal person. Anyway, I'll bring you up in conversation and see what she says."

"Really? Thanks. I didn't want to say anything to Justin, because it would just be weird."

"You've got that right."

"Do you like how I got him to invite you into his tent?" She grinned.

"It's not like that. He thinks of me like a little sister."

"Yet, intelligent people have been known to change their thinking when presented with evidence to the contrary of their previous ideas."

I snorted. "Was I that obvious?"

"Maybe just a little, but he didn't notice, so you'll have to make him take notice."

While the idea had merit, I knew myself. This was nothing short of a gourmet recipe for disaster.

www.ingramcontent.com/pod-product-compliance
Lightning Source LLC
Chambersburg PA
CBHW020252130626
46549CB00005B/2179